BLISTER

AND
OTHER STORIES

BLISTER
AND
OTHER STORIES

BY
BRIAN BISWAS

OBIE BOOKS

The following stories were previously published: "A Sea Voyage" in *Café Irreal*, 2021; "Apologia du Amore" in *Dream Fantasy International*, 2000; "The Meaning of Jealousy" in *Skive*, 2013; "Julie's Murderer" in *Bewildering Stories*, 2011; "Rhonda's Story" in *Crimson Streets*, 2017; "Others" in *Lost Worlds*, 1994; "A Matter of Principle" in *Bewildering Stories*, 2012; "Skipping Stones" in *Daily Love*, 2011; "Mario Bakar" in *Yesteryear*, 2010; "A Love Story" in *Skive*, 2008; "The House in the Forest" in *Skive*, 2007; "Rosé Clare, A Life" part one (as "Gwenedine") in *Anotherrealm*, 2005, part two (as "Happiness") in *Anotherrealm*, 2005, reprinted in *Tien Ve*, 2013, part three (as "The Vulture") in *Mind in Motion*, 1997, reprinted in *Tien Ve*, 2013, part four (as "The Looking Glass") in *Dream Fantasy International*, 2008; "The Town That Went to Sleep" in *Word Riot*, 2004; "A Soldier's Lament" in *Dream Fantasy International*, 2002.

Cover art by Kim Dingwall.

ISBN 979-8-9876259-0-3
Library of Congress Control Number: 2023904594

Copyright © 2024 by the author. All rights reserved.

Published by Obie Books, Chapel Hill, North Carolina. First edition February, 2024.

Praise for Brian Biswas

Praise for *Blister and Other Stories*

"Brian Biswas is a literary mage. He can take the base materials of a historical romance, or a contemporary love affair, or a seagoing adventure, and make them dance in the fairy light of the Uncanny Valley. The titles of the stories in this, his newest collection, give you an idea of their eldritch intentions: 'Julie's Murderer,' 'The House in the Forest,' 'The Town that Went to Sleep.' These are modern folktales. The sheer variety in the book is astonishing, worthy of a Scheherazade, and, indeed, the master storyteller herself is invoked in 'Twelve Nights and a Night.' The final story is a witty updating of Kafka, via Lewis Carroll. Storytelling is Biswas' calling card; he understands the power of Story, with a capital S. Read him because he is a master artificer, utilizing a prose that is both pellucid and shimmering." – Corey Mesler, author *of Cock-a-Hoop*, and *The World is Neither Stacked for Nor Against You: Selected Short Stories*

". . . each story compellingly puts its characters in tough spots that prove to be both gloomy and unexpected." – *Kirkus Reviews*

". . . inventive, genre-blending, briskly paced, tales with elements of the speculative, magical realism, and social critique . . . The best of Biswas's often fable-like tales achieve a thought-provoking depth." – *Booklife*

Praise for *The Astronomer*

"In Brian Biswas' novel, *The Astronomer*, he has chosen to confound us frequently regarding how he and the main character regard reality, and we are often forced to think about our own ways of looking at the real and the fantastic, about fact and fiction. . . . He also challenges us to think about whether or not the dreams and other mental wanderings of people who don't have 'normal' mental lives constitute another reality as well." – Alice Whittenburg, *The Cafe Irreal*

"Biswas' writing is remarkably expansive throughout, and readers will find it deeply impressive how he captures two distinct voices: one of prosaic reason and another of disordered brilliance. Overall, it's a fantastically strange novel that's as grippingly eccentric as the protagonist at its center." – *Kirkus Reviews*

Praise for *A Betrayal and Other Stories*

"Fans of Night Gallery, The Twilight Zone, vintage science fiction, magical realism, irrealism, and—well, fans of good stories and good literature—you need to get your hands on this beautiful volume." – Carol Kean, *Perihelion Science Fiction*

"A debut collection mixes horror and sci-fi—short stories laden with bizarre creatures, life on other planets, and homicidal proclivities . . . Consistently eerie tales that readers aren't likely to forget." – *Kirkus Reviews*

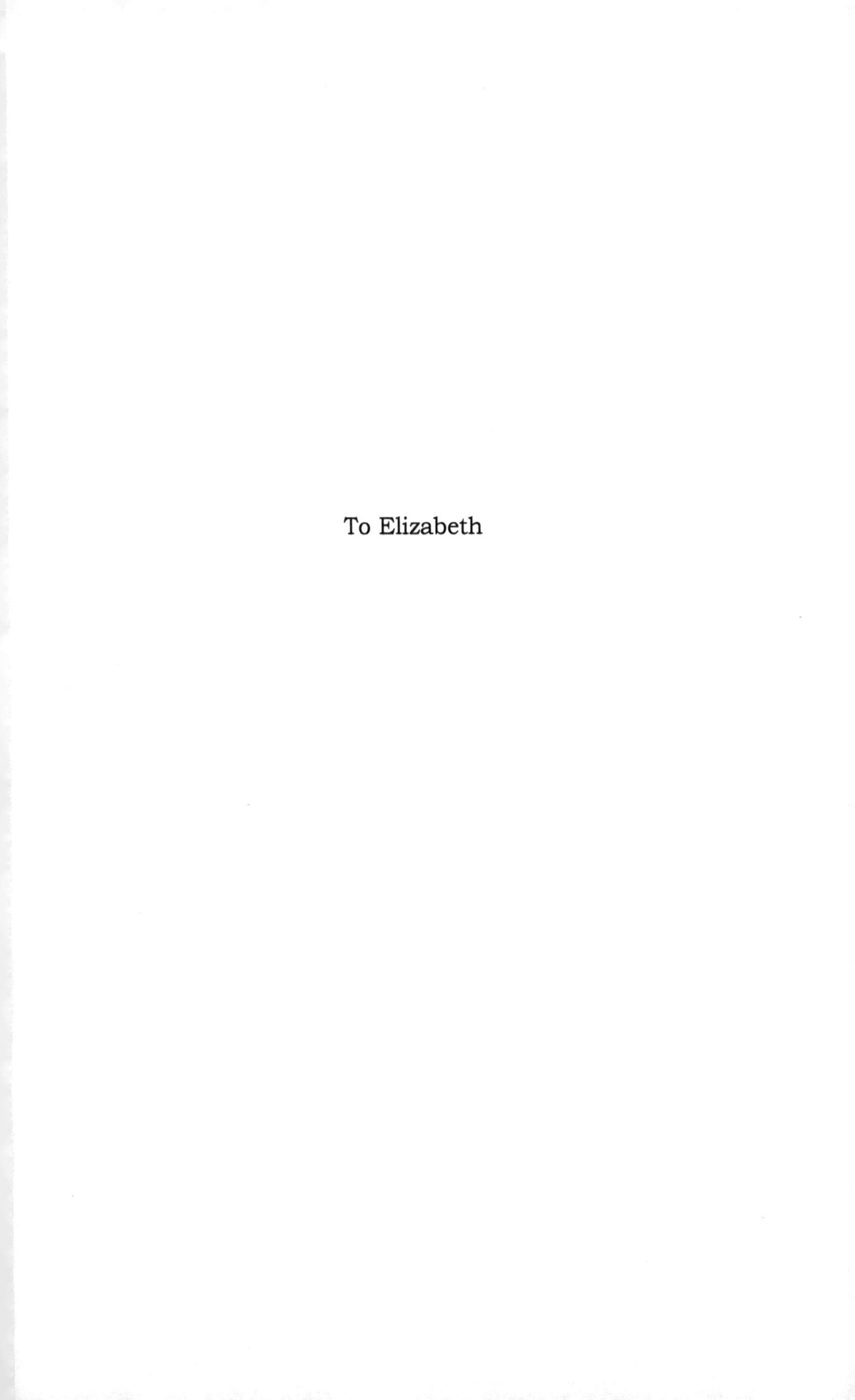

To Elizabeth

CONTENTS

Preface............xi

A Sea Voyage............3

Blister............7

Twelve Nights and a Night............17

Swimming in the Ocean is Wrong............37

The Snowbank............49

Apologia du Amore............63

The Meaning of Jealousy............67

Julie's Murderer............77

Rhonda's Story............85

Others............95

A Matter of Principle............105

Skipping Stones............125

Mario Bakar............133

Two Brief Love Stories............141

The House in the Forest............147

Rosé Clare, A Life............153

The Town That Went to Sleep............165

A Soldier's Lament............177

Richard Court: The Priest, The Sinner............183

Perfect............189

What Happened to Vincent Gutbomb One Day 203

About the Author............225

Preface

The stories in this collection are examples of magical realism. Nowadays publishers plaster that term on all sorts of books, from fantasy to science fiction, but I use the term in its original sense of "a story with many pointers to an unknown meaning." Everything in such a story could happen only it wouldn't happen, not in this world. (In other words, no flying carpets or fire-breathing dragons or otherworldly aliens, etc . . .) It's basically a realistic story but with one or two magical elements, elements the characters take as normal but which give the reader an unsettled feeling, as if something isn't quite right, elements that leave him thinking: "I thought I knew what was going on, but now I'm not so sure. What's happening? I'm not where I thought I was!"

I've also attempted to tell an overarching story. In this I've undoubtably failed, but the idea was: start with a piece that sets the stage ("A Sea Voyage," wherein the narrator describes a chaotic and confusing world), follow with stories that explore the various styles of magical realism, told in a variety of ways—stories about stories, stories wherein other stories are told, stories that are themselves commented upon—and conclude with a piece ("What Happened to Vincent Gutbomb One Day"—in some ways the most realistic piece but in others the most absurd) wherein all is revealed.

BLISTER

A SEA VOYAGE

The storm had been building in intensity for a long time. Far too long, the sailors thought. The ship would have to give at some point—and probably soon. The old square rigger rocked fore and aft, tossed by twenty-foot waves like a cork on the ocean. The torrential rain had long ago drenched everything in sight, the winds having swept away all unsecured objects. The captain, however, appeared unconcerned; indeed, he seemed not even to be aware of the storm! A giant of a man, with a round face and puffy cheeks, blond hair and fiery light-blue eyes, he swaggered up and down the deck like a carnival barker, all the while shouting orders to his crew:

"Rip that sail! Lower that mast! Crowd that boom and bring her astern! Scrub that deck—yes, you Powderboy; scrub it hard—hard till it leaks! Catch that crow! Squawk that fish! Feed that gull with a broiled salmon and make me a coat of fine Persian leather! Move it boys; we've no time to waste. Hey, you! Yes, you with the hammer—let's move it—pound the bulwarks—beat 'em to a pulp—beat 'em till they're fine as gunpowder. And you! Powderboy! I said hammer!—hammer that deck till she springs a leak. You in the crow's nest. Yes, you Crowboy!—let's not dilly-dally! Look to the horizon!—And watch out for the enemy!—We can't be caught with our defenses down and our bulwarks open. Now wait! What's going on? We're off course! Helmsman!-helmsman!! The ship is drifting—due to your bungling. I said hard—hard—hard-a-lee! You men! I never said you could rest. Let's move it; back to work. I want to hear ribs cracking, backs breaking! We're not running a carnival. Let's go!—hey, sailor, off with that straw hat. Wipe that smile off your face. All of you! I want to see frowns, hear curses—break your backs! Doughboy!—Jettison that bilge! Let's move it—I've got a ship to run—and to run soundly. Helmsman! Let's try it again. Hard-a-lee!—"

But in the end it was the storm that gave way (or was it only a lull before the final, cataclysmic event?). The captain looked fore and aft, surveying the damage to his ship: the yardarm of the mizzenmast, having been snapped by the wind, had fallen onto the captain's cabin, smashing the roof to pieces; the rigging of all three masts was in tatters, the sails ripped to shreds. The ship's rails were twisted into grotesque shapes and in several places had been sheared away. Pools of saltwater were everywhere. But did the captain realize what had happened? Apparently not: he made no comments, gave no orders, concerning the storm's destruction; instead, he approached the tiller, pushed the helmsman aside, and with his right index finger began steering the ship, absent-mindedly, this way and that, like a crazy buffoon!

Just then one of the sailors uttered an excited cry. He had spotted a waterspout churning on the horizon. It was shaped like a pillar with ropelike tubes extending horizontally like the arms of an octopus. Its blue gray funnel was the width of fifty ships—and it was drawing near. Shouldn't the captain be worried? Soon the ship might be smashed to bits and they would perish. Wasn't there something the captain could do?

"Heave the anchor, sailor!" replied the captain. He gave control of the tiller to the helmsman and started back down the deck. "Heave it with a grin! And you—Powderkeg—unfurl the sails! Raise the masts! Free that boom! C'mon sailors, let's move it! Pound the decks! Climb the rigging!! And you—helmsman—set a course and abandon it! Crowboy!—watch for gulls! Let's glue our eyes to the sea!"

"What's this?!"—The captain had stumbled over some rope coiled on the deck—"What's this?! A dead man?? Impossible! Hey you—Doughboy—what's a dead man doing aboard my ship? Heave him overboard, I say! Heave him with a grin! Into the mouth of the ocean. I'll have no dead men aboard my ship! Hey you—Powderkeg—that mast is crooked! Straighten that mast!"

One of the sailors, ever obedient to his commander's orders, however absurd they might be, picked up the rope and cast it into the sea. And then, like a lemming, the man cast himself into the sea, and quickly disappeared beneath the waves. But no one paid him any mind. In fact, the rest of the crew seemed half-asleep: strange, silent men lost on the deck of a ship that was itself lost at sea. Perhaps it was the heat, or the eerie green sky, or the feeling of doom that hung over the ship like a fog, which caused their soporific state. Or perhaps it was the captain's lack of direction in dealing with the crisis at hand. "Heaven is upon us! Heaven is upon us!" they cried. "Fear not, ye men of little faith, for Heaven is upon us!"

And you watch it all, from the confines of your cabin, in disbelief and with mounting fear; this is not what you expected to find on your first sea voyage. These are not seasoned professionals delicately guiding the ship through changing waters, over troubled seas, but poor charlatans, crazy hucksters, inept bunglers, unable to live much less pilot a ship, and it is all you can do not to burst into tears, to keep your face pressed against the porthole, to hope against hope that, yes, the gods are looking favorably upon you this day, and that somehow, someway, you will make it safely into port.

BLISTER

Her husband, Paul Neville, was a dashing man. Six-feet-four with jet-black hair and soft green eyes. A ruddy complexion. He was twenty-two years old, born in Dundee, a town in the Scottish eastern central Lowlands, in 1846.

The sea had been Paul's destiny. A cruel and heartless place, it embodied his hopes and dreams. And fears. Over the past decade, in the unruly waters of the Atlantic, over a hundred ships had perished, two thousand souls. Storms came and went with no regard for mankind. And the ocean floor was a watery grave.

An only child, tragedy was nothing new to Paul. His parents perished in the great influenza epidemic of 1854. He had been raised by his grandparents on his mother's side. They were kind and gentle folk but belonged to a generation twice removed from his own. Life with them seemed dull, with little hope of adventure. And so, when Paul came of age and was able to enter the merchant class, he jumped at the chance.

One spring morning—the year was 1868—Paul set forth from Aberdeen Harbor aboard the *Windhover*. It was his fifth voyage. The *Windhover* was a full-rigged clipper ship of over eight hundred net register tons, two hundred feet in length. Three masts rose into a cerulean sky. Sails billowed in the wind. There was a creak and groaning of timbers and foam splashed against the hull.

They were bound for the eastern coast of Australia, a route of fourteen thousand miles, down the Atlantic Ocean and around the Cape of Good Hope, into the roaring forties—strong headwinds that blew out of the west and caused heavy seas—and across the Indian Ocean to Australia. It was a four-month journey, over one of the most treacherous routes in the world.

At Sydney they would load their vessel with grain and wool then return via the same route, tacking as far south as possible, and being careful to avoid icebergs which were known to inhabit the icy waters. Stops were planned along the coast of Africa, where Paul enjoyed trading with the locals whom he found both friendly and clever, then the final leg back to the British Isles.

* * *

It was a beautiful day, with a strong breeze blowing out of the north. Upon leaving port, the men examined the rigging, scrubbed and washed down decks, and filled the scuttlebutt with fresh water. All day long they toiled with hardly ever a break, tarring, greasing, oiling, varnishing, and painting the ship. They drew, knotted, and spun yarn; furled, braced, and trimmed the sails; repaired and replaced the chafing gear. At night they lay amidships or upon the forecastle, smoking, singing sea shanties, and telling boastful tales.

It was an adventurous life, but a hard one. Living quarters were cramped as they were on all vessels of that time, and because sailors considered it unlucky to bathe at sea, the stench below decks became nauseating. The sailors' diet was monotonous: salted meat, sea biscuits, and sauerkraut; rum, mixed with lemon or lime juice to prevent scurvy, was distributed at every meal. Flogging was routine for even minor transgressions, and keelhauling, though recently outlawed, was not an unknown occurrence. It was not long before the men began to grumble.

As it was, none of that mattered. Two weeks after

they left Britain, the *Windhover* was caught in a ferocious storm off the coast of Africa near Greenbacks Shoals. Forty-foot waves and howling winds. They didn't have a chance.

When Sarah received word of her husband's death, she bit her lower lip, ever so slightly. The sea would take him when it wished, she told herself. She must be stoic. Anyway, there was nothing she could have done to forestall that dreadful day. They had been married two years and had no children. It was for this, and not her husband's death, as difficult as that was to endure, that she could not find it in her heart to forgive the raging waters.

Sarah knew Paul's death would not change her wedding vows, that there would never be another. She'd known it from the moment she'd laid eyes upon him. There was never any question. On the inside of her wedding band were inscribed the words: "I shall never marry again."

Luckily, the voyage was insured and Sarah was relieved knowing her finances would be taken care of. Even so, her heart was filled with sorrow. Life seemed to have lost all meaning.

One sweltering summer day in the year of 1869 a blister appeared on her left heel. It was good-sized, an inch in diameter and painful to the touch. She had no idea how she had gotten it. Her shoes were the normal comfortable pair. She had done nothing which might have irritated the area. A bite from a diseased arachnid? It did not seem likely. In fact, it was unlike anything she had ever seen. She covered the blister with a bandage, but a week later it had not improved. In fact, it had doubled in size and taken on a purplish hue, with dark-red spidery veins.

The doctor told Sarah it was nothing to worry about. He gave her an ointment to relieve the soreness. "Morning and night; you'll be fine in a week," he said.

A week later her foot ached and there were purple spots on her heel. The next day maggots were swarming in the wound.

"It's infected," the doctor said when she returned. "What did you do?"

It seemed to Sarah as if he was admonishing her. "Why, nothing," she replied, avoiding his gaze.

"I see." He paused. "It's been over a year since your husband passed?"

"A year and several months."

"Perhaps, then, that is why."

"I don't understand."

"Maggots are indicative of a festering condition." The doctor stroked his chin. "The mourning time has passed. Have you considered taking up with another?"

Sarah's eyes grew fiery. "I made a vow. I will never marry again."

She left his office in a huff.

The next day the progress of the infection mysteriously halted. Though it still had a purplish hue, the foot no longer ached. The maggots had vanished. Sarah sighed in relief.

With money from the insurance settlement, Sarah purchased a cottage in the countryside outside of Kirkwall, a town in the Orkney Islands, an archipelago off the northeastern coast of Scotland. It was a quaint place. There was a cozy bedroom with a twin bed. A living room with an antique fireplace along the central wall. A dining area. A small, but functional, kitchen. She furnished the place handsomely with her favorite belongings, including a rustic table constructed from African woods, a table acquired by Paul on his first visit to Africa and of which he had been so proud.

Eventually Sarah's foot healed, allowing her to venture out for walks to the sandstone cliffs that overlooked the sea.

There she would stay for hours, gazing at the salty deep. Her appearances became the talk of the town, and the townspeople's murmured confabulations hinted at the onset of a madness which seemed destined to consume her.

It mattered not to the young men of Kirkwall. Sarah was in the flush of her beauty. Twenty-one years old, she had sparkling light-blue eyes, a flawless complexion, and luscious red hair that fell in waves to her waist. She must have been sculpted by the mighty gods, they said, for her perfumed skin emitted an intoxicating aroma. An aura of the divine seemed to hang over her, an everlasting light which may have emanated from the heavens and on moonlit nights was clearly visible as an angel's halo.

She received invitations to dinner or social events, all of which she politely refused. Some men were more insistent than others, but it did not matter. She had made a promise to Paul—and to herself—and it was a promise she would keep.

As the years went by her madness seemed to deepen; at least that is what the townspeople said. There must have been a cold, dark secret in her past. Perhaps it involved a fatal lover's tryst?

When Sarah turned twenty-six—more beautiful than ever—the whispering turned into a mocking chorus. The woman was demented, insisted Theodore Croon, a councilman of Kirkwall. Tragedies happened all the time. Even to the man to whom a woman had pledged her heart. One must simply accept fate and move on.

Unfortunately, Sarah's blister turned out to be a chronic condition. She was simply unable to get over the death of her husband! On the harshest of nights she beheld the stain of her despair as it crept back upon her. She locked herself in her cottage and was visible only on moonlit nights, restlessly pacing amongst the shadows. Come back to me, Paul, she thought. Come back.

It was now clear to the townspeople that Sarah's love belonged to a higher realm, and they came to accept this woman who had come into their midst. Their concern for her sanity turned into pity for her loss. Her time at the sandstone cliffs only increased. Sheepherders observed her at Sandy Overlook lost in silent meditation. She expects the sea to return her dead husband one day, they whispered. In truth, she found the views of the sea—Paul's graveyard—comforting: the wide expanse, the peaceful blue waters.

Over time all things are accepted, if we are lucky, and though Sarah's heart was weary she eventually came to accept her fate. It did not lessen the loss, but it did lessen the pain.

The townspeople brought her life's necessities: groceries, clothes, books to read, as well as news of local events to which she listened politely. As the months passed, however, their visits decreased in frequency, until one day only a young woman came, once a week, with food.

Anne was a lovely seventeen-year-old, with French-braided pigtails and luminous dark-brown eyes. Sarah and Anne took an immediate liking to each other. Anne listened enraptured to Sarah's tales of the mighty sea, tales Paul had told Sarah when he returned from the clipper ship *Leander*'s maiden voyage to the African coast. It had been his first journey.

At the time, Paul was a lad of nineteen, a seaman. Upon his return from the African nation of Senegal in the fall of 1865, Sarah Burns and Paul Neville happened upon each other as they sauntered down the wharf at Aberdeen. He cut a majestic figure in his wool pea jacket and bright-red cap, sharply cut flannel pants, and fine rubber shoes. Her eyes locked onto his, she told Anne with a sigh; she resolved to spend her days wooing this man whom it was her destiny to love. He seemed taken by her youthful innocence, she was entranced by his lust for adventure. Their adventure together, she hoped, would never end.

When he proposed, one balmy April day, she was overcome with joy. It was all he could do to temper her emotions. Being the wife of a seaman would be difficult, he said. He would be gone for months at a time, a seaman's life was hazardous at best, and who knew when the sea might claim him? It mattered not, she said, as she threw her arms around him, hugging him with all the strength her slender body possessed.

"Are you certain?" he asked, gently extricating himself from her arms, his eyes fixed on the blue waters of the harbor.

"Of course," she replied, smiling demurely. "You must never doubt my love."

Later, as they snuggled before a roaring fire in his room on Front Street, he told stories of the African coast, of the people there and of his fascination with their culture. Someday, he said, she would journey with him to that magical land. But for now he was comforted knowing his affairs in Aberdeen would be properly taken care of by her.

And as Sarah recalled the tale, Anne sitting wide-eyed before her, her eyes clouded over with sorrow.

One evening, as Sarah was telling stories by a roaring fire, Anne noticed a blister on Sarah's heel. This recurrence was of considerable size, pink in the middle and bright red around the edges.

"Wherever did that come from?" Anne asked.

"It's nothing," Sarah said with a shrug. "Nothing but the remains of a wound from long ago."

"It looks recent."

"Only because of the memory. Which never dies."

Anne blushed. "He must have been quite handsome."

"He was."

As the months wore on, Anne's visits grew less frequent—now she had a young man of her own—until one day her deliveries were left at Sarah's door. Sometimes there was a note of goodwill, a note that grew terser as time passed. But eventually, even those were abandoned.

* * *

It was a sweltering summer day in Sarah's thirtieth year. Because of the heat, her walk that afternoon was short, out to the fields adjacent to the old pine groves. She listened to the plaintive calls of the doves and the bull-finches, saw a trio of buzzards flying overhead, watched with fascination as wispy cirrus clouds twisted into strange serpentine shapes.

The letter was waiting for her when she returned home. It was weather-beaten and had a Senegal postmark. She recognized the handwriting, his peculiar scrawl. It contained a simple message. Inquiring. Wishing her well. That was all.

Her face turned purple with rage as shock swept over her. Her husband had survived! But why contact her after all this time? Was it guilt? Regret? Or something else? She scoured the memories of their early days, looking for a clue, however small, which might have led her to question her husband's motivations, but she came up with nothing. She concluded that he had never really loved her. There had only been an appreciation of the convenience she provided, a wife at home to manage his affairs. She shuddered at the thought. And then she threw the note away.

Sarah's anger gradually dissipated, but she could not deny the feeling of emptiness that slowly built within her breast, an icy coldness that poisoned her with the dregs of despair. It was as if the blister had consumed her, the years between then and now drained of all substance and meaning. As if time had collapsed upon itself or burst and was no more. And it was then she realized that when you were in love, time and love were the same thing and that when one vanished the other did as well.

She bit her lower lip, drawing blood. Knowing what she had to do. Knowing what was now ordained.

At nine the following morning, she went out to the cliffs for what would be the final time. She removed her wedding ring and tossed it into the ocean. She took off her sandals and saw that her foot had healed once again. This time for good. If only the doctor could see it now, she thought.

Her ascension to Heaven followed shortly thereafter.

The next day the townspeople noticed a strange light that seemed to hover over the cliffs, soft and serene, almost celestial in nature, but having forgotten that the poor woman even existed, they had no idea what to make of it.

TWELVE NIGHTS AND A NIGHT

It always begins that way, doesn't it? It always begins at the beginning. And this time would prove to be no exception.

Sophia Rodriguez was nineteen years old, a pretty girl with a freckled complexion, curly red hair and big, round, pale-blue eyes. She had just finished her two o'clock class at Northeastern University in Boston, Massachusetts, where she was a sophomore majoring in comparative literature. It was an overcast day in late October, humid, with a threat of rain in the air. She walked down Huntington Avenue, turned right at the light onto Forsyth Street, and stopped at Tatte's Bakery for a raspberry doughnut—her favorite—then down Forsyth and right again onto Hemenway Street, with its towering oak trees and stately residence halls. She was heading back to her dorm room in Loftman Hall.

As Sophia walked along she thought about the afternoon class she had just attended: Studies in Medieval Middle Eastern Literature. A dozen students were analyzing the *Arabian Nights* (Antoine Galland's translation of 1704). Sophia herself preferred crime novels and mysteries, eschewing far-fetched tales of genies and magic carpet rides, but she simply loved the instructor, Professor Robert J. McMullen. He was tall and thin with wavy, light-brown hair, delicate hands, and dark, penetrating eyes—she could not take her eyes off him—and after reading the work's initial chapter she found herself intrigued by its quaint mix of archaic phraseology and romance.

The book consisted of a thousand and one folk tales linked by a frame story where a woman named Scheherazade bargained for her life with a sultan named Shahryar. McMullen said frame stories were a literary technique and could be employed for a variety of effects. In the case of the *Arabian Nights*, it was used to bind together separate and often far-flung tales, giving form to the entire work. This is how it unfolded: one day Shahryar discovered that his wife had been unfaithful. He strangled her in a fit of anger, then hunted down and killed her lover. Even then Shahryar's hatred of women was not quenched: he resolved to repeatedly marry and then kill his bride on their wedding night. When Scheherazade realized what was happening, she convinced her father to let her marry the sultan. "I have a plan that will save us," she said. "It's quite simple: I'll tell the sultan captivating tale after captivating tale until, at some point, he forgets his evil machinations and releases us."

Sophia had to admire Scheherazade for her ingenuity. And she would never forget when Professor McMullen read the opening passages of the first story: "The Tale of the Ox and the Donkey." His voice was deep and resonant and held her spellbound.

That night while reading in bed, Sophia marveled at Scheherazade's tale of the mariner Sinbad the Sailor. Of how, after spending the riches left him by his father, the lad had set sail to rebuild his fortune. He anchored near what he thought was an island but which was really a sleeping whale on which trees had taken root. He instructed the sailors to wait while he went ashore. When Sinbad landed, the whale awakened and immediately sounded. Thinking their leader had perished, the men set sail, abandoning him. By the grace of God, Sinbad washed up on an island where he had to use his wits to survive.

Sophia was unable to put the book down and, before the night was through, she had read all seven of the sailor's magical voyages.

She was jolted from her reverie by a cool breeze which brushed against her rosy cheeks. It swirled around her like a ballerina and scattered the fallen leaves. She walked under a darkening sky, heard the thrumming of cars as they sped by, the ring of a bicycle bell. She was heading down Hemenway Street, mulling over Sinbad's adventures, when tragedy struck. Without warning, a hirsute hand reached out, grabbed her by the arm, clapped a hand over her mouth, and pulled her into the shadows of an alleyway.

And in that instant her life was changed forever.

* * *

When she came to she found herself in a dilapidated log cabin. She was lying on a tattered green couch. There was a single window, shut tight. Cobwebs hung from a timber ceiling. A clock on one wall ticked loudly.

There was a rickety table in front of the couch and chairs on either side and a man was sitting on one of the chairs and he was looking at Sophia. Mid-thirties, she thought. He was heavyset, with a round, unshaven face, large black eyes, a pug nose. Curly black hair fell to the collar of a red plaid shirt.

The man coughed. "How do you feel?"

Sophia was silent. She was trembling, her heart racing, her stomach knotted in fear.

"I'm sorry," he continued. "I had no choice."

Why me? she thought. She was too terrified to speak. The sweat around her neck grew cold. How had it happened? Her mind traced the circuit of her memories but came up with nothing. There was only the horror of her kidnapping. She saw it once again, in her mind's eye, as he closed in upon her, his face veiled by shadow and mist.

Eventually, she drummed up the courage to ask, "Who are you?"

"I'm your abductor," he replied matter-of-factly.

She sighed. "I see."

The man rose. He drew his face close to hers. She felt his rancid breath on her skin.

"What are you going to do to me?" she asked.

"I don't know," he said.

He really doesn't know, she thought. Her brow was creased with worry.

The man said, "What's your name?"

"Sophia," she sputtered.

"Sophia what?"

"Sophia. Just Sophia." Her lower lip quivered. "It doesn't really matter."

"I guess not," he said. His breathing was slow and steady.

"What's yours?"

"My what?"

"Your name?"

He smiled. "Bill."

"Oh."

The man—Bill—seemed to be studying her. Sinuous lines crisscrossed his forehead and his face had an ominous expression. She listened to the ticking of the clock. It seemed as if the room itself was breathing, slow and steady.

"Why?" she asked.

"Why what?"

"Why did you do it?"

"Snatch you?"

"Yes."

"You're pretty." He stared at her with a yearning look.

She took a deep breath.

Bill paced uneasily about, his black leather shoes clipping the floor. He glanced at her, uneasily as well. He opened his mouth as if to speak but must have thought better of it for he said nothing. An oppressive silence hung in the air.

"I'm thirsty," Sophia said. "Can I have something to drink?"

Bill nodded. He went into another room. She heard ice dropping into a glass. A refrigerator door opening and closing. He came back with a glass that contained a light-brown liquid, iced tea perhaps. "Here," he said. "Drink."

She did.

* * *

Moments later Sophia was fast asleep, dreaming. She was in a sun-drenched meadow, lying on her back looking up at a blue sky. She saw not a single cloud, heard not a sound. And then she was talking to herself, or rather, she was having a conversation with her *Arabian Nights* instructor whom she'd conjured. They were discussing the story of Aladdin and his magic lamp. She shuddered when he recited the part where Aladdin is trapped in a cave by an evil sorcerer and death seemed imminent. A deeper sleep must have overtaken her, for the next thing she knew she heard the coo of a morning dove and her eyelids were fluttering open. She yawned, rubbed her eyes—and recoiled in horror. Bill was hovering over her, a butcher knife in his left hand. The light of the morning sun coming in through the window cast a soft light on his face.

"What's that for?" she stammered and then her face turned red as she realized the stupidity of her words.

"Cutting," he said. His voice was steeped in gloom.

A low moan escaped her lips, a moan she could not have suppressed even if she had wanted to. "Oh, no!"

There was sweat on Bill's brow, as if he might be nervous, or so she hoped, and she saw that his left hand was firm. But it was the look in his eyes which led her thoughts in a different direction. A faraway look, a look of loneliness.

He doesn't want to kill me, she thought. He wants something else. Maybe he really is lonely. Or perhaps he just wants companionship. That and nothing more. He looks lonely, though. He looks as if he hasn't a friend in the world.

"What do you want from me?" she asked.

He waved the knife before her eyes, rocked steadily on his feet. "Tell me . . ." he mumbled. "Tell me a story."

Sophia could not stifle a laugh. Those were the last words she expected to hear! "Tell you a story?" she said. "How can I do that when you're about to slit my throat?"

He put the knife on the table.

"Better?"

She nodded.

He shook his fist and fire flashed in his eyes. "Begin!"

What was she to do? What was she to say? She needed to formulate a plan and quickly, but she had no idea what. Her mind could no longer comprehend what was transpiring.

"I'm waiting. . . ."

The wheels in her mind spun. Her mind thought back to the day before and the day before that. If only—

"All right," she said, the words tumbling out in a torrent. "I'll tell you a story. But on one condition: let *it* decide my fate."

Bill wrinkled up his brow. "What do you mean?"

"If you like my story, I'm free to go."

Bill laughed. "Just like that?"

"Just like that."

"Aren't you forgetting who the captor is here?"

She eyed him with curiosity, saw a hint of a smile, a smile that made crescent curves across bloodless cheeks. "I don't think so," she said. "If you are the captor, then what does a night's delay matter? If you don't like my story, you're free to take my life at any time. But if *I* am the captor, as may instead be true, then it's to your advantage to hear my story and delay for a night what may be in store for *you*."

Bill laughed, a boisterous laugh that seemed to come from deep within his belly. "No, it's *you* who are mistaken," he said. "Your fate was decided long ago." He picked up the knife, waved it once again before her eyes, touched his finger to the blade, then drew it back abruptly. "I wonder what this will look like when it's covered with your blood?"

Sophia didn't believe him, but she couldn't tell him that of course, and so she looked away, wincing as if in pain.

"However," Bill continued, "it might prove entertaining. So be it. Let's hear your story and then I'll decide." And now it was the wheels in his mind which were turning. "But one story isn't enough. No, I want to hear a dozen—or more! If you can entertain me for twelve days I *might* set you free."

She smiled; she loved telling stories. And really, what other recourse was there? "I can ask no more," she said.

"I must run an errand first," Bill said abruptly. "I assure you there's no way to escape; so, please, don't try." He left her then, exiting the cabin and locking the door behind him. She went to the window, looked out and saw him disappear into a thicket of pine trees, trees which in the early morning light cast pale shadows on the earth. She was in the countryside apparently. The yard was littered with scrub brush and other debris. She saw an old stone well, woods, and a sky that towered above.

In the cabin it was as silent as a stone. She tried to open the window then saw that it had a keyed lock. She looked around for another way to escape, but there was none. What if Bill never came back? she thought. What if she were to die out here in this cabin in the woods, never to be found, her bones one day turned to dust? She shuddered. She went back to the window and looked up at a metallic sky. She saw no sign of her abductor. Where might he have gone? And why? Her head began to ache, a dull, throbbing pain. She went back to the couch, lay down and soon was fast asleep.

She was awoken by a noise outside. She rose, went to the window and saw Bill carrying a stack of wood and a small package. She watched as he approached the cabin. Her dark eyes welled with fear.

He unlocked the door and entered. "For you," he said, holding out the package. She unwrapped it and saw that it was a loaf of bread. Sesame, her favorite. And a doughnut. A raspberry doughnut.

"However did you know?" she said, blushing.

"I've watched you for some time."

"Oh."

Bill went into the kitchen and came back with a glass of milk and a slice of bread, toasted and buttered. "Are you ready?" he said. "With your story." He sat down in one of the chairs and looked at her expectantly.

She recoiled in horror as the enormity of the task hit her like a freight train. She glanced at the clock, saw that it was 7:30. Where had the time gone! Once again she had to think—and quickly too—to conjure from her past a story she could now recite. There was one she remembered, but it was from long ago, and if the words failed to impress. . . . She shuddered at the thought.

She looked at him uncomprehendingly. "Why are you doing this?" she said.

Silence. Then simply, "Proceed."

"Now?"

"Now."

She took a deep breath, closed her eyes. And then she began, her voice soft and timid, but growing steadier as the sentences flowed. She recited a story she had told herself many times over the course of a lonely adolescence. On moonlit nights when she was wondering where her own life might lead. "Lifeboat" was the first of several she had written. It was about a young woman sailing across the Atlantic on an ocean liner bound for Spain. The woman had fallen on hard times, having recently suffered through a bitter divorce. Her mind in tatters, she found herself unable to work and took a leave of absence from her job as a financial accountant. She fell into the blackest of depressions, stayed in her apartment for weeks at a time, until one day she realized she couldn't go on like this. She booked her cruise the next day.

As luck would have it the woman got more than she bargained for. One day after the ship set sail, it was caught in a ferocious storm and ended up adrift several miles off the coast of Bermuda. A second ship was sent out to ferry the passengers and crew to the island where they spent several days before boarding a third ship, this one, like the first, headed for Spain. She would never forget the day the ship set sail. Would it take her to a better life in another land? The unexpected happened yet again, this time in the middle of the Atlantic. She was stricken with dysentery and confined to her cabin for days, nursed back to health by a handsome, young doctor with windswept eyes. She fell in love with him—and he with her—and they married after landing at Gibraltar, moving several months later to Australia—the man was from Melbourne—where they lived happily for sixty-odd years.

"Life takes many turns," Sophia concluded. "One never knows where it may lead. Even in the darkest of times, there may soon be light."

"A delightful tale!" Bill cried when she had finished. He clapped heartily. "I want to hear another!" He shot her a mischievous look.

She breathed a sigh of relief. Her face and hands were perspiring, her heart pounding. It was all she could do not to burst into tears.

"Yes, I must hear another," Bill continued. He rubbed his eyes and yawned. "But not tonight." He pointed to a door which led to another room, a room Sophia had not noticed before. "There's a cot in that room where you can rest. I won't disturb you. May the next story also meet with my approval, for if it does not—" He looked at her starkly. There was no need to wonder what his countenance concealed.

* * *

"My tale this evening is an allegory," Sophia said on the second night. "I call it, 'Tranquility.' The protagonist is a remarkable woman, as I'm sure you'll agree. I knew her once. But it was in another place. And long ago. This story is narrated by one of her suitors. A man who could be any man. You, perhaps."

She told a story of an insurance salesman. He was forty years old, plain-looking, with a rather boring personality, and thus of not the slightest interest to women. Or that is what he had always believed. One day a woman entered his office who intrigued him. She had an eccentric personality, a wicked sense of humor, and was also quite pretty. She told him she wanted to take out a five hundred-thousand-dollar term life insurance policy on her husband. After the transaction was completed, the man hemmed and hawed, wanting to prolong their conversation. But she was married and, he feared, would not have been interested in him regardless. So nothing came of it and she went on her way. She did, however, notice his interest and, if the truth be told, found him intriguing as well: soft-spoken with a look of quiet desperation, the mirror opposite of her loutish husband from whom her love had evaporated long ago.

She returned to the office three months later to take out a second five hundred-thousand-dollar life insurance policy. Again, on her husband. She did this every three months for the next year. When the principal reached two million dollars, and the premiums were quite high, the man asked if she knew what she was doing. "I'm waiting to see how high the price on my husband's head must be," she said, "before you kill him and run away with me."

The two of them did run off together—though no murder was committed—and they lived happily ever after.

"Such rollicking fun!" Bill cried. "However, it leaves me much to think about. . . ." He eyed Sophia warily and scratched his chin as if wondering whether her stories concealed deeper meanings.

"Indeed," she replied. "It should."

* * *

"Nothing lasts forever," Sophia said, "which leads me to tonight's story. It's another love story. I wonder sometimes if all stories are love stories, endless repetitions of that most holy of themes. I put myself in this story because . . . well, I know this must sound odd . . . but I feel like I'm in one now. And I may be. One never knows.

"'Excalibur' is the name of tonight's story. It's a magical tale. Sometimes I think the entirety of life is a search for magic. In this case—in this story's case—the search for a magic knife."

Bill smiled and his eyes seemed to shimmer.

"Once upon a time in a faraway land"—she began—"there lived a woman named Faith. She was anything but faithful. Even so, she was not a bad woman. She simply adored men! Her husband ignored her, and had for many years, and so one day she took matters into her own hands, seducing a young man named Sin who was the son of the mayor of the town, a sprawling metropolis on the southern coast of Spain.

"Unfortunately for Faith, news of her lascivious ways soon became the talk of the town. When her husband realized he had been cuckolded, he talked to Sin's father—the mayor—and before the day was out, Faith was arrested, convicted, and flogged in the village square! As you can imagine, Sin was not happy, for he truly loved Faith, and so he confronted his father, who admitted the part he had played in her downfall. 'It was for your own good, my son,' he said. But when he saw the spark of love in his offspring's eyes, he regretted his actions. Unfortunately, there was nothing he could do to remedy matters, for he was indebted to Faith's husband, who had given him a considerable sum to ensure his election.

"Sin thought long and hard, and he agonized for days. Then one night, he realized the only way out of his predicament. . . .

"And it really was easy, Sin told Faith days later, as they boarded an ocean liner bound for America. Faith's husband never saw the knife coming until it was too late. By law, his fortune passed to Faith, who, at the direction of Sin, gave a portion to his father so he could sustain his mayoral position. And everyone was pleased. Faith and Sin disappeared across the sea and lived happily ever after. The End."

"An interesting tale," Bill remarked when Sophia finished. "But I must admit I'm perplexed. Sin loved Faith, that much is clear, but did she love him?—that, I take it, is your point. It seems just as likely—does it not?—that Faith saw Sin as her way out of a marriage she'd grown to despise. And if that's true, then their affair is based not on love but convenience and I see nothing but troubling times ahead. Wouldn't you agree?"

Sophia frowned. "It's not for the storyteller to tell the meaning of her tale," she playfully admonished.

"Of course. Nevertheless, I find it troubling. This question of love. How does one know when one is in love . . . and when one is not?"

* * *

And so it went for eleven nights. But on the twelfth night, the final night, Bill seemed preoccupied. The hope she had harbored—that he might one day change his mind—had all but vanished. As the days passed he had become grimmer, his interest in her—or in the game—seemed to weaken. Most likely, she thought, he had decided how she would die, what end must befall her, but had yet to summon the courage to carry out the act. She did not know how death would come, of course. And if the truth be told she no longer wanted to know, wanted only to tell her tales, night after night. Until eternity came.

There was a fire burning in the fireplace that evening, slow and steady, and Sophia watched as Bill stared vacantly into the flames. He was sitting in a chair some distance from her. His hands were serpented with blue veins on which the firelight flickered. All at once he rose and went to the fire, took the poker and stirred the log until it blazed brightly. Then he put the poker back in its stand and sat down. Sophia was seated on the couch, the pages of tonight's story neatly arranged on her lap. She kicked off her sandals, swung her feet onto the couch, and picked up the first page. He turned and looked into her eyes. Waiting.

"Let me end as I began," she said, "on this the twelfth night. My final night alive, I'm afraid. This story is called 'The Execution.'"

A subtle nod.

"And it so came to be"—she began—"long ago in a small town in Central Persia that there lived a man and his wife and their three sons. The couple were shopkeepers who sold rugs imported from China, rugs of all sizes, shapes, and colors. People came from far and wide and not only to sample their inventory. These shopkeepers were wizards, you see. And if the price was right they would cast a spell on the rug of choice and turn it into a flying carpet. Soon they were fabulously wealthy. Two of their sons became doctors, married, and embarked upon successful careers of their own, but the third son was a layabout. He dropped out of school, took on odd jobs but was fired from all of them. Unable to support himself, he moved back in with his parents who were quickly filled with despair.

"Nothing they did could get him to change his laggardly ways. They employed him in the shop as a stock boy, that is, until they arrived one morning and discovered that the shelves were bare. They sent him to the local seminary for religious instruction, but he was expelled a month later for ridiculing the sacred texts. They thought of arranging a marriage between him and a woman with a good dowry, but quickly came to their senses: no female would give him so much as a glance."

At this point, Sophia's narrative was interrupted by a knock on the door. Bill sprang up and herded her into the bedroom. "Say not a word," he whispered. "If you value your life."

Returning to the living room, he opened the door, finding himself face-to-face with a member of the law: a tall, thin man, with steely grey eyes.

"Greetings, officer," Bill said. "How can I help you?"

The officer eyed him warily and glanced around the cabin. "Missing person," he said. "A woman by the name of Sophia Rodriguez. Age, nineteen. Student at Northeastern. Five feet four. Red hair, blue eyes. No distinguishing markings. Last seen wearing a white blouse, yellow skirt, and sandals. Seen her?"

"Nope," Bill lied. "I've been hiking for days. Haven't seen her or anyone else. Been snatched?"

"Two weeks ago, or thereabouts." He eyed Bill warily.

"People run away," Bill said. "Happens all the time."

"You live alone?"

"You could say that."

"What have you been up to lately?"

Bill paused. "None of your business."

The officer coughed. "We have a case to close, mister. And I'd say you're acting suspicious. Perhaps you're our man?"

"Like I said—"

"You know, it doesn't really matter what you said. We have a crime to solve and . . . Mind if I look out back?"

"Nothing there."

"Then you've nothing to fear." The officer glanced around the room one last time. His eyes settled on Sophia's sandals. An eyebrow raised. "You'll let us know if you see her?"

Bill's eyes narrowed. "Of course."

"Good day."

The officer tipped his hat. "Like I said, I just want to take a look outside and then I'll be on my way." He turned and went through the doorway onto the front porch, looked up at the pine trees that were waving gently against a lowering sky.

Bill went over to the fireplace, picked up the poker and jabbed at the embers. He looked tense. His eyes glowed with a strange light. He went onto the porch and shut the door behind him. He saw the officer by the well and started towards him. The woods trembled. Night closed in.

Fifteen minutes later Bill opened the door to Sophia's room. "It's okay," he said. "He's gone."

She emerged from the room and sat down on the couch. "Who was it?" she asked.

"The sheriff. We won't see him again."

She took a drink from her cup and was about to continue the tale, when Bill interrupted:

"Why didn't you cry out? You could have, you know."

She looked confused. "I don't know," she said. "Really, I don't." And then the thought surged through her and light shot out of her eyes like light from a volcano. "Perhaps no one was there!" she cried. "I wouldn't be surprised if you tricked me. You were testing me, weren't you? You've *been* testing me. All along."

"Now, now," Bill said. "Nothing of the sort. Though maybe it *was* a test. For both of us. Does it matter? No. What matters is your story, your words, and the implication of those words. It's those things, and those alone, that should concern us."

Sophia nodded. He could be so disarming. "And so it came to pass"—she continued, taking up the story's thread once again—"that the father reached a boiling point and one day ordered his son out of the house. An argument ensued; blows were exchanged. The wife was forced to intervene and received a glancing blow. She stumbled, hit her head on a railing, and fell to the floor. She did not rise and appeared to breathe no longer.

"When the son realized what had happened, he fled the house, and presumably the province as well, for he was never seen or heard from again.

"'It was an extreme measure to take, I suppose,' the wife said to her husband when the son was gone. 'But it had to be done.' The woman had been an actress in her youth, you see, and had merely been playing a part.

"'Yes,' her husband replied, 'all is well once more.' And taking this as a sign from above, they sold their business and retired to a town on the coast of the Mediterranean Sea where they lived happily ever after."

"An intriguing tale," Bill said, "and one which, like all your stories, gives me much to think about. Even so . . . I'm still not sure what to do. About you, I mean." His face darkened as he drifted away in thought. . . . "However, I have the night to contemplate your fate. *Tomorrow* I shall deliver my verdict."

He left her then, exiting the cabin with a weary sigh. She heard the click of the lock. And she knew that, one way or another, her fate was sealed.

* * *

"You're allotted one more tale," Bill said on this the thirteenth night. "The problem is I simply can't make up my mind! This time, however, will be different: unlike the previous nights where you had a day to prepare, this story will be improvised."

Sophia was on the couch, lying on her side, her feet propped on a pillow. She was tired and there were dark circles under her eyes, the days having exhausted her. Bill had always treated her well, it wasn't that, but the strain simply had become too much.

He stood before her now, an imposing figure. "All your previous tales have been musings on love," he said, "and this story—this final story—may be on that topic as well, but let it be longer than the others. Recite it and I will pronounce judgment."

Sophia's heart was beating like a drum. Her hands were shaking. She took a deep breath, counted silently— one, two, three—a ritual she'd performed to calm her nerves since childhood—and then began. "My last tale," she said, "is a story about a man and a young woman and what came between them. A story which—perhaps— may bring us both salvation."

(In truth, this was a story Sophia had composed long ago, one night when the stars were out and the moon was full and her thoughts would not still.)

"Once upon a time there was a man and a young woman whom he coveted. One day he decided he could not live without her and he spirited her away to a cabin in the woods where he was set to make her his wife."

Suddenly Sophia uttered a cry and swooned.

"Is something wrong?" Bill gasped. His eyes darted frantically. He rushed into the kitchen, emerging moments later with a glass which he held out for her.

Sophia forced a smile, took a sip. She looked at him and he at her. Her body trembled.

"Thank you," she said. "I don't know what came over me." She paused. "I'm sorry, Bill, but I must stop. I'll let *you* finish this tale."

And with that she collapsed on the couch, the couch from which she'd recited her twelve tales of love. Her body weary, her spirit still, she had no idea how this final story would be received.

As if from afar, came a clarion call: "Hi, ho! Hi, ho! What a marvelous tale!" And as Sophia looked at him through misty eyes, she saw—or thought she saw—a sprightly lad of no more than eighteen, his face unblemished, his long brown hair flowing free. "You're free, my dear," he said. "You've acquitted yourself well!"

And Sophia could not help but observe that he was beaming. "I'm free to go?" she said, unable to believe his words.

"You're free to go."

It was as if a weight had been lifted from her shoulders and she burst into tears, sobs as sudden as April showers. "I can leave?"

"That's what I said, isn't it?"

She sighed, closed her eyes, and before she realized what had happened, had drifted off to sleep.

* * *

When she awoke the next morning her abductor was nowhere to be seen. The window, now open, let in golden sunshine. She tried not to think about what had happened in the log cabin, wanted only to leave, to return to school, and quickly, too, and quickly to forget. Yet what could be more enchanting than the tale she now could tell?

She opened the door and started down the moss-covered path that led away from the cabin. But something was wrong, a gnawing sensation that tugged at her heart and would not let her go. She knew Bill was lonely, in his own way he was as lonely as she. And how could she abandon him when he had set her free? It was ludicrous, of course—and it *was* ludicrous—her feelings in this moment, and yet would it be too much to ask, she wondered, if she returned one day to the cabin in the woods and told a fourteenth tale? And perhaps a fifteenth. He would have liked nothing more!

But, no, she would never return, would never come back to recite another tale, even if she wished she couldn't have done so, for when she turned to look at her place of imprisonment for a final time she saw that it had vanished, swept away as if by a magical wind. She shut her eyes tightly, stifling tears, imagining not her fate as it might have been but his at it was before she emerged out of her dream world now dissolving and plunged headlong into a clearing which had opened before her, tumbling headlong into a blinding and everlasting light.

SWIMMING IN THE OCEAN IS WRONG

If you could have one gift, what would it be?" Ned was speaking to his wife, Ingrid, one evening after dinner as they sat on the couch in the living room.

She thought for a moment, said nothing. He took up her hands.

"Anything. Just dream."

"Oh, nothing," she said. "I have you, dear. There's nothing else I need or want."

He smiled. "I could say the same about you, of course. Think. There must be something."

Ned and Ingrid Watkins were in their mid-twenties, had been married just over a year. He worked as an insurer for the state of Georgia. She was a children's librarian. An attractive woman with long, wavy red hair and light green eyes; her face was freckled, her nose thin, and there was a dimple on her left cheek. Ned was short and thin, brown hair, brown eyes, clean shaven, a hint of a smile on his lips. It was, Ingrid often teased, a mischievous smile which she had always found alluring.

Even though both had paying jobs, their combined income barely qualified as middle-class. They were able to pay the bills but with little leftover. And it was this that prompted Ned's question.

"Well . . ." Ingrid began, slowly drawing out the word, "there's one thing, I suppose. . . . Oh, Ned, you'll make fun of me for asking—"

"Never!" he said. "There's nothing I could deny you." He paused, then added with words so soft that only he could hear, "or rather there's nothing I would deny—if only we had more."

"I'd love a bathing suit, Neddie!" She blurted out the words. "In my favorite color: turquoise blue. One piece, of course." She blushed. "I'd dance in the waves!"

Ned, it must be said, was taken aback by his wife's admission. She rarely approached the water; why, she did not even know how to swim! "That's rather ordinary," he replied. "And hardly special. Surely there's something else that suits your fancy."

"I've had my eye on a designer suit at the Purple Puddle," she continued. "It's just the color and style I want and is trimmed with gold. It's been in their window for the longest time. Last week I went inside to have a closer look. I caressed the material; it's elegant. I looked at other suits but I've fallen in love with this one. Unfortunately, I saw the five-hundred-dollar price tag and—"

Ned's eyes widened. "I see."

Ingrid realized, of course, the impossibility of their ever making such a purchase. Moreover, she felt guilty at putting her husband in the position of having to deny her what she craved. "Please forget I mentioned it," she said. "It was only a passing fancy. I don't know what got into me."

* * *

They said no more about the bathing suit that day or in the days that followed, but the conversation left Ned troubled. A pit formed in his stomach, worthlessness clouded his mind. Two weeks later he tried bringing the subject up, but Ingrid shunted it aside. So he let the matter drop.

Ned's office was located in downtown Savannah, a vibrant place with enticing boutiques, bookstores, and cafes. To save money, He usually brought his lunch—Ingrid packed it in a paper bag which she put in his backpack—and when the weather was nice he took his backpack and went to a nearby park to eat. He enjoyed taking walks around the area afterwards, observing people, shoppers mostly, and window-gazing. On this day—it was a sunny Tuesday in mid-June—he was walking down Lincoln Street when he came upon it: The Purple Puddle. He had never noticed the place. It was small, but quaint. He wondered about the coincidence, then realized he had probably passed by many times. He peered in. Two young women were examining clothes. A third person, a fashionably dressed woman whom he assumed was the shop keeper, was speaking to them. As he gazed through the window, he could not help but admire the clothes. And then he saw what must have been the suit his wife desired. A cut so daring it took his breath away. And the color was divine. She certainly had exquisite taste.

He opened the door and went inside.

* * *

The shop owner was ringing up the ladies' purchases. One of the women turned towards him and smiled. He shuffled his feet. He had never been in a women's boutique before and felt self-conscious.

"Be with you in a minute," the owner said.

He went over to the swimsuit area and examined the items. They were pricey, that was for sure, though none were as expensive as the suit Ingrid had asked for. Unfortunately, neither were they as becoming. He thought again of the suit in the window. The one his wife desired. . . .

"Hello, sir. I'm Cindy. How can I help you?" The woman had a pleasant smile. The badge on her blouse read: Cindy Blacock. Proprietress.

Ned heard the rattle of the front door as the customers left. He glanced around the store and saw that no one else was there. His eyes settled on the owner. She looked to be in her early thirties, had curly blond hair, bright, eager eyes, and was wearing a blue pants suit and a white cashmere sweater.

"I'm looking for a present for my wife," he said and added, "something not too expensive. . . ."

Cindy smiled. "What did you have in mind?"

"A bathing suit. One piece."

The woman ushered him to another aisle. "You're in luck," she said. We have a good selection. Is there a particular designer she favors?"

"I'm not sure."

"Well, no matter. We carry only the highest quality. What size is she?"

"Eight, I believe," he said.

"Over here." Cindy took him to the end of the aisle and showed him several suits. One was pink with an embroidered white band. Seventy-five dollars. He fingered the material. Like satin.

"I'll take this one," he said. "It's a bit over my price range, but I think we'll manage."

"She must be very special," the lady said.

Ned blushed. "She is." He handed her the suit. As she was turning to go wrap his purchase, he said, "Wait! I was mistaken. Ingrid's a size six. Yes, I'm certain. She used to be an eight, but . . . She's very proud, you know. Of her new figure, I mean. Is it possible—"

The woman looked through the suits. "This seems to be the only one of this model on display," she said. "Let me check in the back."

She left and he was alone. He looked towards the window display, pondering. And then he made his decision. He went to the display and removed the five-hundred-dollar suit. He examined the tag. Size six. He breathed a sigh of relief. He folded the suit and put it in his backpack. He was turning to go when he realized that this left an empty stand in the window. He cursed his lack of forethought. Praying he could fix things before Cindy returned, he rushed back to the swimsuits, pulled out a one-piece, and put it on the empty display stand. Voila! He took out his handkerchief and wiped his brow. He was sweating profusely and his heart was beating rapidly, but he had accomplished what he had set out to do. His beloved wife would be overjoyed, and, even if the theft was discovered, his purchase of another suit ensured that he, Ned Watkins, would not be suspected.

Cindy returned, a frown on her face. "I'm sorry, sir," she said, "but we don't have your wife's size in that suit. I checked the inventory; they're on backorder. They should be in in two weeks. I'll set one aside for you—"

Ned froze, thought quickly. He had not anticipated this. "That won't do," he replied. I need to get her something today. You see, our anniversary is tomorrow."

"How about this one?" she said. She held up a flaming-red two-piece. "Size six. It's not the style you were looking for, but it's one of our most elegant. Perhaps your wife would like to try something different . . . for this occasion, I mean."

Ned did not hesitate. "Perfect!" he cried. "She'll love the color *and* the style." He paused. "How much?"

"Let's see . . ." Cindy searched for the price tag. "You're in luck, sir. Seventy-five as well."

"Wrap it up!"

When this was done, he thanked her and, complimenting her on the quality of her merchandise, promised he would return one day. Then he left the shop, almost bumping into a couple who were entering. "Excuse me," he said, and quickly averted his gaze.

* * *

"Ned, you didn't have to get me anything."

They had just finished dinner and were seated at the dining room table. A small white box wrapped with a red and blue ribbon lay in Ingrid's lap.

"Open it," Ned said.

"But—"

"Please." He smiled.

She undid the ribbons and lifted the lid, no more than an inch. "Ned—"

"Come now. It's not as if this is Pandora's Box."

"All right, then." She opened the lid fully and saw a wrapped item. She removed the tissue paper. And then she saw the bathing suit, the blue satin material, and her eyes opened wide. "Ned!" she exclaimed. "You shouldn't have! I mean, we can't afford—"

He dismissed her objection with a wave of his hand. "Don't worry, dear. They were having a sale and anyway there's a bit extra coming in this month from the Ferguson contract."

"Even so, we couldn't possibly afford—"

"It's taken care of." His words were firm. He had never spoken to her like that and she found it odd that he did so now, but she did not reply.

She held the suit up for both of them to admire. She rubbed it against her face.

"It's the one you wanted, isn't it? And the right size?"

She examined the label. "Yes," she said. "It's perfect."

He looked relieved. "Put it on."

She rose, clutching the suit to her chest. "If you insist!"

"I'll do the dishes while you change." He picked up the plates and took them into the kitchen. She went into the bedroom, emerging minutes later in her new suit. "What do you think?"

Ned gasped. His wife had never looked more beautiful, not even on their wedding day. "Simply stunning," he said. "I'm at a loss for words."

She turned around so that he could view the suit from all angles. "It fits perfectly," she said. And then she hesitated. "But, dear—"

"Think no more about it," he interrupted. "We can afford something special once in a while."

She went back into the bedroom and he finished loading the dishwasher. Ten minutes later they were on the couch in the living room. He took up her hands. "How about we go out to North Beach tomorrow? You can wear the new suit. I'll be the envy of the men!"

She laughed. "And I can dance in the waves."

"As you've always wanted."

"As I've always wanted. . . ."

Ned smiled, but his expression hid a troubled mind. He could not deny that what he had done was wrong. And deceitful. Then again, he *had* patronized the store. And he would do so again once their finances improved. It was his pesky conscience that was troubling him. But wasn't that to be expected? After all, he was a moral man.

"Honey?" It was Ingrid, breaking his concentration. "Are you okay? Your eyes look glazed."

"Nothing, dear," he answered, wiping his hand across a sweaty brow. "A hard day at the office. I'm glad it's Friday. Tomorrow will be better—a trip to the beach for two!"

* * *

"Here?"

"No. Over there." Ingrid pointed to an open section of beach closer to the water.

Ned spread the blanket. Ingrid carried the picnic-basket, set it down next to the blanket. She unfurled her towel and spread it on top of the blanket. Then she plopped down, legs extended. He went back to the car and returned moments later with the beach umbrella and two chairs. He opened the umbrella and thrust it into the sand. It was 11 a.m. and the sun blared in a cloudless sky.

Ingrid was wearing a yellow coverup over her new suit. Her red hair glowed in the soft rays of the sun. She looked out over a sea that reflected the deep-blue sky. She saw a motorboat in the distance. She rose, stepped out of her flip-flops, and went down to the water. She put a toe in; it was pleasantly warm.

Ned was seated in the beach chair. He saw Ingrid at the water's edge, looking out over the ocean. She looked so happy. He smiled. He gazed up and down the shoreline. North Beach was a three-mile strip of paradise on Tybee Island offering stunning views of the Atlantic Ocean. He saw sea birds hopping down the shore, stopping every few feet to peck at the sand. The ocean was calm and there was only the hint of a breeze.

Ingrid came back to their blanket.

"Going in?" he asked.

She sat down in her chair under the umbrella. "In a bit."

He rubbed his stomach.

"Getting hungry?" she asked.

"It's the sea air," he said. "Gets my appetite up every time."

She laughed. "I could use a drink," she said.

Ned spied the concession stand about thirty yards away and started towards it. "Back in a minute."

Cumulus clouds were visible near the horizon. Ingrid watched as they moved slowly to the south. She saw two children, a boy and girl, playing in the sand nearby. One of them saw her gazing and said, "We're building a castle, lady. Want to watch?"

Ingrid smiled and went over to the children. She sat down on the sand. "What do we have here?" she said pointing at a rectangular hole, perhaps a foot deep. There was a bucket filled with water which the children were using to wet the sand. They raised the castle walls, molding them with trowels. The girl took a stick and cut out a section of one wall for a doorway, which she lined with pebbles. Ingrid admired the children's attentiveness and remembered her time as a child on Cape Cod.

After fifteen minutes, she realized Ned had not returned. She looked over at the concession stand. No one was there. She frowned—but then she saw her husband nearby talking to a lady who looked to be in her early thirties, wearing a stylish blue-and-gold bikini. The woman looked familiar. She thought for a moment and then she remembered—the owner of the Purple Puddle, Cindy Blacock! Ingrid had met her when she wandered into the store once to look over their selection of bathing suits.

And she noticed something else. Her husband, her dear, sweet Ned, seemed . . . apprehensive. Ingrid was too far away to hear a word that was said, but she noticed that the woman was doing most of the talking. Ned was shuffling his feet, his usually buoyant expression replaced by one of worry. At one point he looked back in her direction, his hands visibly shaking. Was something wrong?

* * *

Cindy was speaking. "We've never had a theft."

Ned blanched. "When did it happen?"

"Just the other day. Luckily, the thief made off with only the one suit. . . ."

"You don't say."

"We're insured, of course, so no problem there, but then again, the insurance company will probably raise our rates."

"I hadn't thought of that," Ned mumbled, then stopped short, realizing his words may have been heard.

"Thought of that? Whatever do you mean?" she asked.

"You're quite right, I mean, that they'll raise your rates."

Cindy nodded. "As I was saying, I tidied up the window display myself that very morning and the suit was there. It didn't sell that day, but when I closed the store at five it was missing. The thief was bold enough to steal it in broad daylight! My, my, what is the world coming to?"

"Oh, dear," Ned interrupted. "I must be going. I promised my wife a drink and I've been gone too long. It's getting hot. . . ."

Cindy brightened. "How does she like that suit you bought the other day? That flaming-red two-piece."

Ned felt sick.

"Where is she?" the lady continued. "I'd love to see how it looks on her."

He looked towards their blanket and umbrella. No one was there. He scanned the beach, his eyes settling on the two children. Their sandcastle loomed.

"I don't see her," he said. "I told her I'd be right back. She must have grown impatient and . . ." His words trailed off.

"I won't keep you any longer then," Cindy said. "She probably went into the water. It's such a lovely day. When you find her and have eaten, drop by our spot"— she pointed further up the beach—"Harold and I will be here all afternoon. I would really like to see her in that suit!"

Ned nodded and hurried away. He returned to their blanket, saw her towel folded neatly. He went down to the water. Two girls were tossing a red beach ball; they laughed when the ball hit the water, showering them with spray. A young man on a boogie board was paddling. A few feet from him there was a mother with her toddler, the child splashing in the water.

"Excuse me, mam," Ned said. "You haven't happened to see my wife, have you?" He described Ingrid and her bathing suit.

The woman pulled the child from the water. "You're in luck," she replied. "I just saw her. And that suit! It was the most beautiful I've ever seen. Clung to her skin as if it had been designed for her. Hey, are you newlyweds? She had that look about her. . . ."

Ned felt relieved. "Where is she?" he asked.

"Why, out there." The woman pointed to a spot farther down the beach about twenty yards out to sea. Only no one was there. "She was coming down the beach and passed in front of me. She was beaming, like I said. She went on ten yards or so and then stopped and looked back. I thought she was waiting for someone but no one came. Or maybe she wanted to see if someone who wanted to see her swim was watching. Eventually she gave up and went out into the water up to her knees. She was wading parallel to the beach—heading away from where we are now—but at one point she turned, dove into the water, and headed out to sea—" The woman smiled. Ned saw her white teeth. White as pearl.

"But she can't swim!" he exclaimed. "She's never been able to swim." An icy chill ran through his body. "Ingrid!" he cried. "Ingrid! Ingrid! Ingrid!"

"Harold, this is Mr. Watkins." Ned turned and saw Cindy Blacock, her husband in tow. "His wife was the lady I was telling you about, the one for whom he bought that flaming-red bikini. You know the suit I mean. I can't wait to see how it looks on her." She turned to face Ned who had been frozen into silence. "Is your wife nearby?" He averted his eyes, looking past Cindy towards their own spot on the beach, now abandoned, and six feet from it a sandcastle, abandoned as well.

He forced out the words, "I'm afraid there's been a misunderstanding. I don't know how it happened. I . . . ." He stood among the three of them open-mouthed, terror lodged in his throat.

"Whatever do you mean?" Cindy asked, a puzzled expression on her face.

The first woman looked confused as well. "A bikini?" she said. "I thought . . . ." Her words trailed off.

Ned turned and scanned an empty sea. No, someone was out there, a black dot drawing near. His heart raced. Perhaps Ingrid had not been paying attention and had ventured too far out. A current might have carried her away. She had never been far from the shore, after all. A rip current would have taken her by surprise. It happened all too often. Why, in her case it was almost inevitable.

A figure loomed, slowly came into focus. Yes, it was a swimmer, or someone attempting to swim. He couldn't be sure. He flapped his arms like a wounded bird in an attempt to draw the swimmer's attention.

"Mr. Watkins, is something wrong?"

And then he realized his dilemma. If it was not her . . . he shuddered at the thought of having lost his beloved. But if it was, what then?

The sun burned high in the sky and there was not a breath of wind.

"Mr. Watkins?"

An answer was expected but he had none. The sun's angry rays clawed at his eyes. The heavy humid air was suffocating. He was conscious only of the waves as they lapped unforgivingly on the shore.

The Snowbank

L ife is full of twists and turns, it's true," I began. "Why, I know a story of a woman whose life began with an amazing adventure. It's the most astonishing story that I've ever heard. Would you like to hear it?"

Charles chuckled, knowing of course that he had no choice. "Do begin," he said. "Your stories amaze me no end."

I went to the kitchen and returned with a bottle of Chardonnay. I uncorked the bottle and poured each of us a glass. I placed a fresh log on the fire. Then I picked up a dozen sheets of notebook paper on my writing desk, filled my pipe, and began.

* * *

The winter of 1918 had been mild in the gently rolling countryside near Chillicothe, Ohio [I read] but this was about to change. The sky was overcast and gray. A blustery wind from the north shook the few pine trees that dotted the farmland.

Mabel Pierce was twenty-two years old, a young mother whose first child, a girl, had been born six months previously. Mabel was a pretty woman, medium-length wavy blond hair, sea-blue eyes, a lightly freckled face that imparted a look of innocence and grace. Jenny was a quiet child who slept twelve hours a day. Her hair, deep brown at birth, was growing much lighter. Her blue eyes had changed to light brown as well. She loved to be rocked and often babbled for minutes on end.

Mabel was startled when, shortly after lunch, the child began coughing fiercely. Her brow was feverish and her eyes glazed.

"Tim, something's wrong with Jenny," Mabel called to her husband. Her face was strained with anxiety. Without waiting for a reply, she added, "The poor girl's burning up!"

Tim was a stocky man with short-cut brown hair and light-brown eyes. He scratched the stubble on his chin. "It's probably nothing," he said. "Let me check . . ." He put his hand on Jenny's forehead. "She *is* a bit warm. But I think you're exaggerating."

"Here," she said, handing her husband a thermometer. "I'll hold her while you take a reading." She took Jenny from the highchair and held her to her bosom, rocked her until she was asleep. Tim put the instrument under Jenny's left arm. He counted off two minutes. "Hmm," he said, as he read the thermometer. "One hundred and two. It looks like you were right."

"Of course, I'm right," Mabel snapped. "I'll call Doctor Fletcher at once."

The family physician lived on the outskirts of Chillicothe, about twenty minutes from their rural home. He'd delivered Jenny at the local hospital and was trusted by them both.

"Aren't you forgetting something," Tim said. "It's Sunday. No one will be at the office."

"I have his home number," Mabel replied. "He said to call day or night."

She was interrupted by a wail from Jenny. "Oh dear," she lamented. "Tim, you simply must call. The number is by the telephone."

He went over to the phone, picked up the receiver, and dialed.

There was static on the line. The doctor's voice sounded far away. "Hello?"

"Dr. Fletcher? It's Tim Pierce. Sorry to bother you. It's about Jenny. She's got quite a fever and, well, Mabel's worried."

He handed the phone to his wife.

"Doctor Fletcher. This is Mabel." Her voice was strained. "Yes, yes. One hundred and two. It came on suddenly. I don't know what to think. I mean, I do know what to think and—"

"Mabel," her husband interrupted. He had gone over to the living room window and was looking outside with alarm. "The snow's started. It's coming down like the devil."

"Yes, doctor. Tim will bring her right over. I appreciate it. I know it's the weekend and . . . your office . . . certainly. He'll be there in half an hour."

She replaced the receiver in its cradle and turned to Tim. "Get the car ready. I'll bundle up Jenny."

Her husband looked pained. He pointed out the window. "Mabel, if it keeps on like this much longer I won't be able to see six feet ahead. How about we wait until morning? I'm sure—"

Mabel shook her head. "Jenny feels hotter than ever. The doctor will know what to do. You'll be fine."

Tim knew it was useless to protest. He went into the bedroom and put on his long johns and thick wool socks and his leather boots. Laced the boots tightly. Mabel went into the hallway and returned with two cotton blankets. She wrapped Jenny up tightly.

They put on their coats and went out to the gravel driveway. The night was chill and raw and a strong wind blew.

Tim started the Model-T.

"Wait a second . . ." Mable said. She went back into the house and returned a minute later with a mug of hot coffee. "This might come in handy." He smiled.

He put the child in the back seat and nestled pillows on either side, looked out across the fields. He had lived in central Ohio his entire life and had never seen snow come down so fast. Big, thick flakes that stuck to the ground. He'd have to hurry. Luckily Beacon's Road led straight into town.

"No dawdling," Mable said. He went outside and cranked up the car. To his relief it started right up. He got in and with a wave headed off.

He was five miles out when an avalanche of flakes cascaded down from the sky. The wind picked up, hurling snow in all directions. He looked over his shoulder at Jenny who—luckily—still was fast asleep. Thank God for that, he thought. The road conditions became so bad that Tim thought about turning around, but he knew that the roads near the city would be in better shape so it was safest to continue.

Gray clouds, heavy as lead, hovered close to the ground, and a noisome wind blasted the vehicle. The car's headlights were practically useless. Tim realized the chances anyone had left the city were slim; even so, he reduced his speed to a crawl and blasted the horn repeatedly to warn anyone who might have ventured out.

There was a cry from the back seat. He turned and saw that Jenny's eyes were opened wide. She was wheezing and coughing worse than ever.

"Be still, Jen," he said softly. "We're almost there."

It was 2:10.

* * *

When Henry Gibson woke on December 14, he had a premonition it would be a difficult day. His bones ached and he felt a throbbing in his temples. He lived on the outskirts of Chillicothe where the Southern Line Railway passed through. The line ran from Wheeling, West Virginia around Chillicothe, through Columbus, and on to Cleveland. Beacon's Road paralleled the tracks, crossing over them on the southern side of town at Max's Crossroads, Henry's station.

Henry worked part-time as a gatekeeper. It was a job he had held for nearly a year, a simple one, but of the utmost importance. In that day and age gatekeepers were posted at crossings to manually raise and lower the gates when a train approached. Due to the extreme length and weight of the gates, they had to be counterbalanced by heavy cast-iron weights at their bases. As a train approached, Henry would crank the gates, which would remain down until the train passed. It was boring, monotonous work, but the stations needed to be manned twenty-four hours a day.

On this day, Henry was in a quandary. It was 2 P.M and his shift ended at 1, but his replacement had yet to arrive. And in this blizzard who knew where the man might be? Probably stuck on the road. Or perhaps the evening train itself had been delayed. Whatever, the guard house was no place for him to wait out a blizzard, certainly not one this ferocious. And if he didn't leave the station now, he'd be forced to spend the night. Already the snow was a foot deep, the drifts three feet or more. And with the rate that snow was falling, who knew what the landscape would look like by morning? He might be trapped here for days.

Henry lived two miles from the station, a twenty-minute walk under normal conditions. He put on his overcoat and left the guard house, locking the door behind him. He looked down the track but could not see more than a dozen feet ahead. "Nothing's coming down that line," he said. With a shrug he started off. It took half an hour to go a quarter mile. The wind howled, assaulting his face. His heart pounded and he grew apprehensive. What if he became disoriented and couldn't make it home, he wondered? What if he died out here and they found his body days later in a snowdrift?

* * *

"We should be in Chillicothe in ten minutes," called out Fred Walpole, conductor of the Detroit Express, as it approached Max's Crossroads. He was speaking to Billy Tilton, the engineer. Tilton gazed out over the landscape at the dark and lowering sky. "And it won't be a minute too soon. Never seen a storm like this."

Though there was little danger to the train, which could plow through the most ferocious of blizzards, Walpole was ill at ease.

"I tried contacting Max's Crossroads," Tilton said. "No answer."

"Guard's probably left." Walpole laughed. "Can't say that I blame him. A man would have to be crazy to be out in this—"

There was a loud crash and a boom. Tilton hit the brakes. "Oh, my God!" he cried. His words could hardly be heard over the howl of the train as it decelerated.

"What in the world—" Walpole clung to the railing. "Did we hit something?"

"There's nothing out here. Or rather, nothing should be—"

"A cow?"

"Are you kidding me? In this storm?"

The train hissed to a halt. Walpole opened a cab window and looked out. A blast of wind hit him in the face and he grimaced.

"See anything?" Tilton asked.

"Nope."

Walpole called to the back of the train. "You men okay? We must have hit something. Everybody out. Assess the damage."

The Detroit Express was steam-powered and hauled twenty thirty-ton coal cars. A crew of six, plus the conductor and engineer.

Tilton radioed the Chillicothe station and told them what had happened. "Struck something," he told the startled radio operator. "At least that's what we assume. Train itself seems to be fine."

Ten minutes later Chuck Rivers, the caboose man, entered the cabin. He was covered head to foot in a layer of thick snow. Frost on a scraggly black beard. He looked terrified. "Better call the police," he said grimly. "Cowcatcher's mangled. And there's glass from a headlight on the track. A light that's not ours."

* * *

Walpole and three crewmen fanned out to search for evidence of a collision. They examined the area in front of the train for a hundred yards but found nothing. Fifteen minutes later they were joined by Commander Swank and four patrolmen who had arrived on the scene. The eight men proceeded ahead slowly, fanning out, their footsteps halted at times by the wintry blast.

Suddenly, two hundred yards from the crossing on the track's eastern side, Officer Benjamin cried out. He had come upon a black Model-T lying on its side. The front of the car had been sheared off, the top crumpled, the windshield shattered. Benjamin radioed Swank and a minute later everyone was on the scene.

"Nobody escaped this," one of the men moaned.

There was a stench of burning metal. Smoke was rising and the sick smell of gas hung in the air. Snow cascaded over the vehicle, covering the metal with big thick flakes. An hour or two longer, Walpole thought, and it would have been hidden.

The driver's side door had been welded shut by the heat of the collision. Looking through shattered glass, Swank saw a limp body against the passenger door. They managed to dislodge enough roof away to expose a hole big enough for Swank to get through. He poked his head inside, expecting the worst.

There was a man in the wreckage. His face was turned away and his left arm was twisted at an odd angle. There was blood on the front seats and blood on the steering wheel and blood on the car floor. Blood was everywhere. Swank had fully pulled himself inside when he saw it. A twitch in the man's right leg. He gasped and called out to the others, "Somebody call an ambulance. The guy's alive." He crawled forward and put his hand on the man's back. The body was warm. "Buddy, can you hear me?"

The right leg twitched a second time. Then the other leg moved and a low moan escaped the man's lips.

"Jesus Christ," Swank exclaimed.

He pulled himself out, called to the men: "Let's get him to Mercy."

Walpole said, "What the hell happened?"

Swank shrugged. "Dunno."

Officer Ray appeared. "The crossing guard's gone," he said. "And the rails are up. You know what that means . . ."

"It means the driver didn't have a chance."

"The crossing guard figured the run was cancelled and wanted to get home before—" one of the men said.

"—before this happened! What kind of professionalism is that? Of all the . . ."

An ambulance appeared, its lights barely visible in the falling snow. Three men jumped out. The opening through which Swank had entered the vehicle was too small to remove the victim, so they cut through the driver's side door and pulled him out that way.

Any internal injuries will kill him, Swank thought as he watched.

The man was moaning. And coughing blood. They put him on a stretcher and loaded him into the ambulance. Swank looked at him lying there. A young man, early twenties, but his face had a wizened look, like a dried apple. Your luck may have just run out, Swank thought. What were you doing out here in this storm anyway?

As if reading his thoughts one of the ambulance men turned to Swank and said, "The guy was probably on his way into town. Thought he could beat the storm. Young man. No brains. Sadly, that's all it takes."

Swank looked at the man with questioning eyes. "Think he'll make it?"

"I doubt it."

The three medical men got back into the ambulance. The driver turned on the siren and the vehicle crept ahead. It made its way back to Max's Crossing where it turned left onto Beacon's Road. The driver looked at his watch. It was 5:30. With luck they'd be at the hospital by six.

"Joe," he said. "Radio Mercy. Tell them we're on our way and that the victim's in bad shape." And with that the driver directed all his attention on the road ahead.

* * *

It turned out that the men were lucky. Just as quickly as the storm had come up it abated, the heavy flakes reduced to intermittent flurries. A full moon could be seen rising in the east and a vague lightness filled the sky.

The driver pushed the ambulance to its limits, pulling into the emergency entrance twenty minutes later. A crew was waiting to take the man to an operating room where his injuries were assessed by Dr. Robert Gulac, the chief of emergency services. The man had severe internal injuries, Gulac said. Multiple organs were failing and broken ribs had punctured both lungs. He would have to operate at once, but the odds were slim. The man died in surgery an hour later.

Back at the accident site one of Swank's men found the vehicle registration in a battered glove compartment. It listed the owner as a Mr. Tim Pierce, 1504 Bluehaven Road. He handed the card to Swank with a grimace. It put a name to the victim. That he was a local man somehow made it even more tragic. Swank called headquarters. They would notify Pierce's wife, if he had one, or a relative, if he didn't. Thank God that wasn't one of his duties.

It turned out that the damage to the train was minimal: the left side of the locomotive was damaged from the impact of Pierce's car, which had struck the train at a sharp angle and careened off, flipping over before settling on its side. Damn, Swank thought. If Pierce had made it to the crossing ten seconds earlier none of this would have happened. Or if the guard hadn't left his post or had put the crossing arm down before he did so. Though—Swank had to admit—Pierce might not have seen the arm in the storm anyway.

"Commander." It was Officer Blue. "Message from headquarters. They just heard from the hospital: Pierce is dead."

Swank cursed under his breath. Then he turned to go. There was nothing more they could do. The night was black as pitch. He kicked angrily at a snowbank, sending clumps of packed snow flying in all directions. The crossing guard would lose his job, that was for sure. It was sad, he supposed, but inevitable. And as for Mrs. Pierce—assuming there was a Mrs. Pierce—that was sad but inevitable, too. Pierce was a young man, maybe with a young'un at home. A wife without a husband. A child without its father. Tragedy everywhere one looked. Swank spat at the frozen ground. He got into his patrol car and started off. He felt leaden with fatigue.

* * *

"Mrs. Pierce?" A call from Mercy. Something about an accident. And a death. The words closed on her like a trap. Her face felt numb, her hands tingled. A hundred needles pricking the skin. "Tomorrow . . . when you can make it in . . . to identify your husband." She trembled and her heart pounded. She could say nothing, do nothing, feel nothing. "We assure you the physicians did everything . . . everything . . . everything . . ." The room spun. Mabel had always been apprehensive by nature and when she hadn't heard from Tim by dinner she had a feeling something might be wrong. The storm—she had never seen the likes of it. And the child's condition . . . Oh God, no, let that not be . . . "My baby!" she cried to a startled hospital official. "What about my baby?"

A gasp. Then, "Oh god—"

* * *

When Mabel hung up the phone, she saw Jenny before her, her only child, surrounded by a halo of light: her dark hair, her fair skin, her bright brown eyes. And thoughts emerged from the folds of her memory. . . .

She gazed into the heart of a dark forest which blotted out the sun. She encountered shivering pines, heard the wind whispering. The air was humid and heavy, her heart was hammering. She heard a siren, a low drawn-out wail, and then the wind was blowing harshly, skirling madly though the trees, and the forest seemed to tremble. . . .

When she realized she was lost in a daydream, she shuddered. Dreams are horrible things, she thought. She felt as if she was drowning and she burst into tears. "No, no, no!" she cried.

* * *

Swank was heading back into town when the call came through: turn around and restart the search. There had been a second passenger, a child. Time was of the essence. He could not believe it at first, didn't see how this day could unleash more bad news. But it had. Yet another death. And a child at that. Misty stars flickered in the anticipatory night.

* * *

It was 9 p.m. Lights from the station at Max's Crossing shone brilliantly over the landscape. Snow was piled high, three feet or more, and there were drifts which must have been twice that. The train clung to the tracks, motionless. Lights blazed in all twenty cars and the locomotive's headlight punched a beam a hundred feet ahead. The track itself was encased in ice and snow, as if holding the train prisoner.

Men from four additional patrol cars joined a frantic search. A dozen weary men fanned out. The snow was crusty; it cracked under the men's boots. The frigid wind sliced into faces, penetrated skin to the bone.

Officer Blue examined Pierce's vehicle once again but found no evidence of a child. It was surmised that the babe must have been thrown clear, only to die of frostbite, which would have come within hours in the frigid cold and that horrid wind that made it all the worse.

* * *

"Commander! Over here!" It was Officer Blue, his voice frantic. He was at the edge of the light beam cast by the locomotive, half-a-dozen yards from where Tim's car had come to rest. Swank rushed over. Blue was near a large snowbank. He was cradling a sack, a puzzled look on his face. As Swank drew near, he saw that it was not a sack, but a blanket. And it enclosed something.

But wait! Why was Blue smiling and rushing towards the ambulance, the ambulance that had just reappeared out of the darkness? He called over to Swank, "It's the child, sir! And it's alive!"

Swank heard the baby's cries. His hands were sweating and his heart pounding. He repeated to himself: how could anything survive in this storm?

Blue handed the baby to a waiting member of the ambulance crew as Swank drew near and clapped him on the shoulder. "How did you find it?" he asked.

"I heard a cry," Blue said. "It was buried in the snowbank. The force of the collision must have hurled it clear. Wrapped in blankets, deep in snow . . . It was a miracle."

"No miracle," Swank said. "The blankets provided warmth. Snow protected it from the wind."

"Even so, it was lucky we found it. It wouldn't have made it through the night."

That was for sure, Swank thought. The sky had clouded over once again and once again the snow was beginning to fall. He felt as if he was drowning in emotion.

Someone in the ambulance called out that the baby, a girl, looked to be in good shape. The poor thing was terrified, of course, and wailing away. Then, its siren blasting, the ambulance started off into the darkness, heading towards Mercy.

On the way back to headquarters, Swank relayed the latest developments. His voice was breathless. His body ached from the night's stress. "I'm heading over to Mercy," he said. "But first, there's one thing left to do."

When he reached the outskirts of Chillicothe, he stopped at police headquarters on Front Street, ignoring the congratulations of Officers Chesterfield, Thurman, and White who surrounded him when he entered the building. He pushed the men aside, rushed to his office, and called the girl's mother. "Mrs. Pierce," he said a moment later. "Good news. The best news! Your little girl is safe. She's on her way to Mercy now. Can you—"

The click of the receiver on the other end indicated that the child's mother was already on her way.

* * *

Jenny Ann Pierce cried relentlessly for three days and nights. On the fourth day she grew quiet and looked up at her mother, a preternatural calm having come over her.

The events of that tragic night were never mentioned. Mabel died when Jenny was eighteen, a victim of the flu. Jenny married an army officer two years later and traveled the world. When she was thirty-five her husband was killed in a military confrontation. The death benefits enabled her to live comfortably. She settled in Barcelona, a place she had come to love. She led a quiet existence, never remarried, and lived to the age of ninety-eight. The announcement of her death was a single line in the local paper:

Jenny Ann Pierce, age ninety-eight, died Tuesday.

Her body was interred three days later.

* * *

A dead silence hung over the room when I finished my tale. I could see that Charles was moved: his face was taut and there was a faraway look in his eyes.

"An intriguing story," he said. "And a sad one. It reminds me of a tragic incident in my own past. Did you know that my great grandmother survived the sinking of the Titanic?"

"Good heavens!" I exclaimed.

"She was six years old. Think about it: had she died my mother would never have been born. *I* never would have been born. And we wouldn't be here—now—having this conversation."

I grunted. "A sobering thought."

"The type of thought that can drive you mad if you think about it too deeply."

"Better, then, that we don't," I said. I picked up the bottle and held it for his inspection. "Another glass of Chardonnay?"

APOLOGIA DU AMORE

Jason waited in the attic of the house in which he had been born. No one could see him. He watched as two men, dressed in military garb, dragged the girl kicking and screaming into the park. She could not have been more than sixteen years old. They stripped her and then the younger man gave her to the older for his pleasure. Her cries echoed throughout the town. Jason watched as the townspeople—men, women, and children—came to their windows and looked on in morbid fascination. A few of the braver ones somehow found it in themselves to venture out into the park. Even though rules were posted on storefronts and lampposts, which specifically prohibited gathering around the condemned as their sentences were carried out, they wanted a closer look, but they were shooed away by a third man (Jason had not noticed him before) wearing a brown vest and trousers and brandishing a whip which he cracked with animal fury.

The park was surrounded on three sides by rows of poplar trees. On the fourth side, the side which faced the house, stood an abandoned well. Once it supplied the town with water, but with the arrival of the modern water system, and its miles and miles of pipes, its intricate pumps, now lay lonely and forgotten. It was rumored to contain skeletons of the executed.

When the old man was finished he looked up at the younger man and grinned. "Want her?" The younger man shook his head, no. The girl's face was terror-stricken, her arms and legs bruised, and there was blood running down her back where the old man had dug in his nails. Once she had been beautiful, like a fairy-tale princess: her blond hair flowing to her waist, her eyes green, her face smooth and clear. But she was not a princess, she was a prostitute (or so the authorities claimed). She had been caught by the authorities outside the city limits, making love with Jason in the meadows, and she was about to be murdered before his eyes.

And then they passed the girl back and forth. And they slapped her. And they called her whore and slut. And the younger man decided that he wanted her after all. And he took her there in the park as the older man cheered.

When the younger man was finished, he threw her to the ground and he bellowed, like a wild animal. A deep sadistic groan from the depths of his hideous soul—Jason thought that was what it sounded like. And Jason knew that no one, not even those (like himself) who were hiding, were safe from the death squads and that love, which had lighted the world for two thousand years, which had been born with the world and would die with the world, would soon be a relic of the past.

They did not even have the decency to blindfold the girl. They kicked her and they laughed. And then the man with the whip came over and flogged her until she was covered with blood. And as Jason looked at the girl in the park and at the men who were murdering her, he saw a likeness to himself being tortured in the attic of the house in which he lay.

The whip-lasher pulled out a pistol and handed it to the younger man, who grinned. Then he put the gun behind the girl's left ear and sent a bullet into her brain. She did not cry out or gasp or do anything, but simply collapsed and lay still. Jason could not look anymore, he covered his eyes and sobbed.

Nor was it any easier when the murdered girl came to Jason that night. "Poor boy," she said, wiping his brow.

"I love you," he said. "But I have failed you. How can you forgive me?"

"You speak of failure," she replied. "But in love there is no failure. Only love."

Jason was silent and he looked at the floor. I am not worthy of you, he thought.

And she wiped his brow. And she stroked his cheek. And she kissed his lips.

Yes, it hadn't been easy, she said, but yes, she'd survived, she'd even seen God the Almighty—though he wasn't as magnificent as people claimed—and now she'd been reborn and she was in another world. But he'd best stop worrying about her and get on with his own life and leave her to the rest of the universe. And then she was gone.

Her green eyes and her long blond hair. She was like a mare that ran through the fields and longed to be free. Jason must love her but he cannot love her but he must. Did she know what it was like to love someone so passionately that your head spun and you were dizzy and you could not think and you could not eat nor sleep and your heart ached with longing? Did she know what that was like? She said that she did, but Jason did not believe her.

It was night when they found her, with Jason in her arms. He had just proclaimed his love to her and she was laughing, but gently for she loved him too. They would love forever, she said, in life and in death, they were but two sides of a golden coin.

How, then, did the authorities find them? There in the meadows. What had they done to lead the death squads to them? "You will be shot!" they exclaimed, in unison, like a squadron of devils. And Jason escaped into the hills and left her to die. To be raped by the devil and to die.

And now she was gone. And Jason had never known her and he would never know her and life was no longer worth living, except for the memories of her and her blond hair and her green eyes (like a wondrous goddess). But it was so filled with pain, the remembrance of her (and not the remembrance of his love for her, that was full of joy), that Jason had to stop and he would think of her no more.

But the memories did not stop. And they would never stop. She was the air that he breathed, the water that he drank, his shelter from the storms of life, from its evils and from its hatred. She must not leave him. Promise him that! She would never go!

And as Jason's memories unfolded, he saw them pull up her dress and throw her to the ground, and then one of the men covered her face to muffle her screams and a second man—the bastard—he raped her and he was laughing as he raped her and he would not stop raping her and Jason wanted to kill him. And then the man with the whip came over and he wanted in on the fun too, he said, and he whipped her until she was nothing but a mass of blood.

It was then that Jason came out of hiding; he had to speak (the park was deserted and he spoke to no one, though he thought he was addressing the executioners: madness had overtaken him): "You cowardly bastards! You cowardly bastards!" he cried and he waited for a barrage of bullets to take his life, but he heard only her cries as they beat her. They are deaf, he thought; how else not to be consumed by their own savagery? And as Jason slunk back into the attic—defeated, alas defeated—he heard the moans of a bull from some far-off place and the roaring of the ocean and the gun ringing out as she shuddered and lay still.

THE MEANING OF JEALOUSY

Jimmy Roberts was fourteen years old. A gangly youth with a winsome face and starry eyes. An infectious smile. A svelte neck dotted with freckles.

"Sarah!" he called to his sister. "You can come in now. But keep your eyes covered."

Breathless with anticipation, Sarah fairly flew into the living room. Jimmy had never seen his younger sister so excited. He grinned from ear-to-ear. She really was charming, as his parents were always telling him. Her freckled face. Her long, blond pigtails. Her bright and eager eyes. Her tenth birthday. Her mother and father seated on the dark-blue satin couch, hand-in-hand, smiling broadly.

"Okay, you can look now."

She opened her eyes. Her hands fell to her sides and she gasped. There before her, illuminated by the sun that was streaming in through the living room window, was a shiny, bright-red two-wheeler, its chrome wheels glistening in the majestic light, the multi-colored streamers that hung from the handlebars reflecting the colors of the rainbow. She could not believe her good fortune. It was just what she had wished for.

"Oh!" She brought her left hand to her mouth and gasped.

"It's what you wanted, isn't it dear?" Her mother's gentle voice.

"Yes, of course," she sobbed. "Thank you. Thank you, everyone. I've never felt so happy."

* * *

On the deck of the cruise ship, *Princess of the Sea*, Sarah looked out over the pellucid ocean. It was 8 a.m. and a pastel sun was rising, casting shimmering beams of early morning light over the water. The ship had set sail from Miami earlier that morning on a seven-day voyage that would take it through the islands of the eastern Caribbean. First stop: San Juan. There would be whale-watching the following day off the coast of St. Thomas. And fireworks that evening. Dancing in the Grand Ballroom. Movies in the Cinemax. The excitement would never stop.

Behind her rose the sun deck from whose vantage point one could best take in the splendor of the ocean. She would go up there, but not today. She smiled to herself as she recalled those happy events from long ago, the glorious adventures the two-wheeler had taken her on. Life had been so easy then. Easy and carefree. She was forty-six years old now. Divorced with no children. Her brother lived across the country in Orange County, California. He had dropped out of the religious college his parents forced him to attend and joined a utopian colony known for its encounters with the law, only to quit six months later and marry an English professor from Cal-Tech whose long, brown hair smelled of rosemary and whose writings had touched his heart. Sarah had not seen him in years. He wrote now and then but said little. Her parents were the children of preachers and devout Christians their entire lives. They prayed fervently for their son's soul but held out little hope for him. Lost in the mists of solitude, they took long walks in the countryside, conversing with God. Sadly, there was never to be a reconciliation: a car accident claimed their lives when Sarah was forty-two.

Sarah was wearing a pleated red dress, white sandals, with a yellow sunbonnet to shade her eyes from the sun. Her skin smelled of orange blossoms, an afterbath lotion a salesman from New Orleans had assured her would one day bring a man of destiny to her side. She was smiling, but there was a hint of sadness in her eyes. Her marriage of three long years was over. She had tried so hard to make everything work out, but in the end it simply fell apart. A bitter separation. A nasty divorce. Her parents would have been disappointed—or rather, angry—but she didn't care. No, that wasn't it. It was simply that she had given up trying to please everyone. Then came the tragedy. And now she desperately needed to get away.

She had saved a thousand dollars over the past year so she could take a trip, alone, to the Caribbean. It was a trip she hoped would revitalize her spirit and wash away the troubles of her past. And now as she gazed into the gentle light of the dawn, saw the sun's crimson rays shimmering on the ocean, she felt as if she was dreaming or had died and gone to heaven.

A light breeze was blowing and it swept her blond hair across her face. She saw a school of dolphins knifing through the water. Exotic seabirds swooping low. She closed her eyes, stuck out her tongue, tasted the salty ocean spray. She listened to the sound of the waves breaking gently against the hull. What pleasant memories it evoked to hear the ocean. There had been a trip to the northeast with her family when she was a teenager. The year before her brother had gone off to college. She remembered the sandy beaches of Cape Cod. Whale-watching off Provincetown. Blueberry picking in Sandwich. It had been so peaceful. She smiled. She hadn't felt this relaxed in a long time.

She opened her eyes and looked up into the sky, at the cumulus clouds, so white and puffy, drifting on a gentle east wind. She stood there awhile, thinking of nothing in particular. And then she looked back at the deck. She saw two women standing by the railing on the port side. She'd seen them several times—always by each other's side, always talking; she assumed they were traveling together. Once they smiled at her, but she had not introduced herself. She had always been shy with strangers. The women were talking animatedly about something or other and she drew close so that she could hear what they were saying. They looked to be in their late twenties. One woman had short curly brown hair, a radiant complexion, thin figure. She was wearing a blue blouse and a bright yellow wraparound skirt. The other woman had long red hair, a round face with light-green eyes, a dimple on her left cheek. She was tall and shapely and was wearing a red blouse and jeans.

"No, it wasn't like that," the brown-haired woman said. "It wasn't like that at all. I never said an unkind word to him. Nor he to me."

"Something must have happened. Or he wouldn't have—"

"Please, Laura, no more questions."

"Was there someone else?"

"Of course not. We drifted apart, that's all."

"I can't believe that, Rachel."

"I'd be lying if I said otherwise."

Sarah felt embarrassed. A love affair gone sour. Her thoughts drifted away. . . .

* * *

"No, Steven, no!" Tears were streaming down her cheeks.

"There's nothing more to say," he replied. "We've been kidding ourselves and you know it."

"How can our marriage mean so little to you?"

"I was drunk. I didn't know what I was doing."

"How could you?"

"We never talk. I was lonely, I guess."

"You guess? We talk all the time, but you never listen."

"No, that's not it! That's not it at all!"

And he was right. That was not the reason. It was something else. Her husband's burning eyes upon her, anger gnawed at her heart. She looked past him, across the room and out the window, at the mauve twilight. He was a handsome man with thick black hair, a raucous laugh, or so she had imagined him to be, and she thought she was in love with him. She had been so young. She had a successful career—she was a corporate lawyer—and his had never worked out. He was jealous of her success. That was the seed that led to their destruction.

* * *

While Sarah was thinking about these events, oblivious to the passing of time, Rachel spied a bird perched on the railing of the sun deck directly above her.

"What a beautiful creature!" she cried. It was two feet long, with white tail feathers, black wing markings and a yellowish bill. It was looking at Rachel and Laura and crying *ticket-ticket, ticket-ticket.*

An avid birdwatcher, Laura said promptly, "A white-tailed tropicbird. It's rare to see one far out at sea."

And before Laura could utter a warning, Rachel sprang on the ladder—marked CREW ONLY in bright orange letters—that led up to the quarterdeck to get closer to the bird. It hopped down the railing as if daring Rachel to follow.

"Laura, he's so pretty!"

"Rachel, get down!"

It was too late. The bird cried again, louder than before, and beat its wings furiously. Then it came directly at Rachel, claws extended, squawking angrily. Rachel moved her head to the right to avoid being clawed, but her left foot slipped off the ladder and then her right and suddenly she was falling and with a cry she tumbled over the railing and into the ocean, her hands grasping at the ephemeral air.

"Rachel, no!"

Sarah spun around. She heard a splash and a siren ringing out and she saw crewmen rushing down the deck. A man exclaimed, "Woman overboard!" One of the crewmen pulled a life preserver from a storage area and threw it over the railing. Another jumped into a lifeboat secured on the port side and Sarah watched as it was lowered into the water. A crowd had gathered and people were peering over the railing—Laura foremost among them. "Everyone back!" one of the crewmen cried.

"There she is! Over there!" someone yelled.

Sarah looked over the railing and saw Rachel, her arms flailing. She saw the waves churning. The white-caps of the waves. There is no way anyone can live in the sea, she thought.

Eventually, the crewman in the lifeboat reached her and he held out his paddle and she grabbed the end and he pulled her on board. Even from this distance Sarah could see that Rachel was crying. The crewman draped a blanket over her and then he turned and began paddling back towards the ship. Sarah turned to see Laura staring glassy-eyed at the ocean and she noticed that her hands were trembling.

* * *

"You never touch me! What's wrong with you?"

Sarah glared at her husband. She had tried to work through her anger at his infidelity. But she could not get over the hurt he had caused. For that she had yet to find forgiveness.

And then one day the final insult: he accused *her* of seeing someone else. She insisted it was not true. He laughed. His face was purple with rage.

"Liar," he grumbled.

She said nothing. He disappeared into the bed-room and when she joined him an hour later—or was it two?—he was fast asleep. But she could not sleep. She lay awake in the darkness gripped by the terrors of the night.

It took a week for her to drum up the courage, but one morning shortly after they awoke she told him she was leaving. Shafts of morning light were breaking through the bedroom window. He was in the bathroom shaving. She was in bed, the blue cotton sheets wrapped tightly around her. She expected him to start yelling, but there was only a morbid silence. She tried to explain herself, the motivations for her actions, but he merely shook his head, a gesture of dismissal. Okay, was all he said.

Thank God they had no children.

* * *

It was not until two days later that she saw the women again. Rachel and Laura and another man who was with them. It was evening and the horizon glowed a faint red. The sea was smooth and clear.

As she drew closer she saw that the man was quite handsome. Young, dark skinned, with large hands and long, slender fingers. Curly, black hair. He was wearing tan pants and a brown plaid shirt open at the collar. A gold bracelet around his right wrist.

"I've always been headstrong," Rachel was saying. She spoke directly to the man who smiled. "But I don't know what came over me this time."

"You wanted a closer look at the sea bird," the man said. "That's all." He spoke with a strong Peruvian accent.

Rachel looked embarrassed. "No, that wasn't it—it was . . . jealousy."

"What do you mean?"

"I wanted to claim the bird." She paused. "It doesn't make any sense, I know."

The man sighed. "Jealousy is a bitter word. It eats away at the heart like acid. I shall never forget the tragic case of Major Blum and his fiancée. Adair Flaxton was a lovely woman with peach-blossom cheeks. Quite a catch for the major. Never had two people seemed so destined to fall in love! But the dashing Sergeant Crumble took center stage and Adair found herself unable to control her feelings and . . ."

The man continued speaking, his words slowly coiling around the women. But they moved further from Sarah and she could no longer make out what he was saying.

She looked out on the infinite sea and listened to the murmuring of the water as if awaiting answers, but none came. The wind was blowing from the south and it seemed to pass right through her body. It was at that moment that she realized her ankles were aching. It was a condition that had plagued her for years. Ever since she and Stephen had begun to self-destruct. Her doctor told her it was stress, nothing to be alarmed about, but in the months before the voyage the aching had become unbearable.

* * *

She was certain it was over then. There would be no more arguments, no more tearful nights. One evening in a fit of anger she burned every picture she had of him and drowned the ashes until they were cold.

She could not have received a greater shock when, a week later, a knock came upon her apartment door and she opened the door and he stood before her. His hands limp at his sides. He looked pale as death. He wanted her back, he said. She did not know of course, but she guessed that his heart was racing.

If this had been the movies she would have slammed the door in his face. Only it wasn't the movies. Maybe she didn't need him, maybe she couldn't stand the sight of him, maybe the very sound of his voice turned her stomach, maybe all of that was true—but still she wanted him. Or, more precisely, she wanted what they'd once had. What they'd lost and would never regain.

And it was the true measure of her desperation when she answered softly, "Come in."

He sat on the aging green couch in the living room, his left leg crossed over the right. His fingers interlocked. His face was ashen, his veined hands gleaming with perspiration. They talked for over an hour. About nothing in particular. He didn't bring up their problems and she didn't want him to. At one point he stared at her intently as if trying to read her mind. He is going to say something about us, she thought. But he said nothing.

"Would you like a cup of coffee?" she asked.

He said that he would.

* * *

They had moved closer. Once again Sarah could hear their words.

"He probably meant to kill himself," the man was saying. "He realized he had lost the woman he cared about more than anyone else in the world and that nothing would bring her back. As far as he was concerned, his life was over."

"No," Rachel countered. "I don't see it that way at all. He didn't want to die. He was desperate."

"What do you mean?"

Rachel paused. "He didn't commit suicide. It was an accident."

The man screwed up his eyes. "An accident? I find that hard to believe. He was an excellent swimmer and the water that day was calm."

"No, you don't understand," Rachel continued. "Maybe he *meant* to take his life. Maybe he was convinced it was the only way he could end the pain. But when he slipped past the reef, felt the warm embrace of the ocean—no, I don't believe he wanted to die. Only it was too late. And the pain at that instant must have been unbearable."

The man shrugged. "It's all the same," he said.

The shriek of the ship's whistle announced the approach of San Juan Harbor. Sarah saw the glittering lights of the city, the winding streets paved with gold, the majestic hill overlooking the harbor. And when she turned back around to bear witness to the end of their conversation, they were nowhere to be seen.

* * *

"I'm sorry it didn't work out. It's my fault. I never meant to hurt you, Sarah. Please—"

She began to cry.

"I am the failure. You are the righteous one."

"No, please."

He rose to go. She saw tears welling in his eyes. "You're right," he said. "It will be better this way."

And then he was gone. Two weeks later he hung himself. He left no note.

* * *

Under a cloudless sky, the ship pulled slowly into the harbor, its bones creaking like a weary ghost. She could feel the waves lapping against the ship's hull and a soft smile played upon her lips. She looked into the eye of a slowly rising sun. Orange flames burned her eyes.

"I shall always remember you," she sighed, but her words were lost on an outlaw breeze that was blowing in from the sea.

It was fifteen minutes before the ship's whistle blew a second time and the passengers began to disembark. She looked back upon the canescent ocean, looked for the women but did not see them, knew she would never see them again, for the winds of the world never blew the same way twice, and then she departed, her spirits lifted by the cool morning air and the unexplainable scent of fresh strawberries that seemed to hang over the harbor, and she hurried down the walkway into the arms of a brave new world.

JULIE'S MURDERER

It is known for certain that when Louis Kincaid happened upon the murder scene and saw his commanding officer, Sergeant O'Neill, hovering over the body of Julie Blain, he in no way suspected O'Neill of murder. The sergeant was an upright man, honest, thoughtful, devoted to his men and his profession and was not the type to commit even a petty crime. But as Kincaid watched O'Neill staring uneasily at Julie's body—a single thrust of a knife had ripped open her chest—he felt himself growing apprehensive, as if, just maybe, O'Neill knew more about the crime than he was letting on.

Kincaid had been returning to his quarters for the night, walking past rows of barracks, when he noticed O'Neill in the pale moonlight, about ten yards in the distance. He called out to the sergeant and was drawing near when he realized that O'Neill was staring not at Julie's body but at a diamond necklace that lay beside it. The diamonds were of an unusual cut—Kincaid could tell so even at this distance, so large were the stones—and Kincaid assumed that robbery was the motive for the crime and that O'Neill must have scared the thief away. When he reached O'Neill, he asked what had happened, but the sergeant—apparently in shock—did not respond. It was then Kincaid recalled rumors that O'Neill had once had an affair with a Miss Blain; the affair—the rumor went—had been intense but had not lasted long. Kincaid had never believed a word of it. It would have been out of character for the man he knew. Just then police cars arrived, their red lights ablaze in the night, and a moment later, cops were everywhere. The murderer had no intention of covering up the crime: several feet from Julie's body, a long butcher knife was found; and nearby, Julie's clothes: a blouse, skirt, and wide-brimmed hat.

"It was only a matter of time," said the chief investigator as he puffed on a cigar. "What did the woman expect, anyway?" A prognathous, contemptuous man, he seemed almost indifferent to the murder. He looked at Kincaid and laughed. "It could have been one of a thousand men," he said. "God knows, she had that many lovers!"

Julie Blain was not a prostitute, but the investigator was, for all practical purposes, correct. It was no secret that Julie enjoyed a rich and varied love life: this was a military base, tension and stress were facts of life, and the men needed the relief that only sexual congress brings. Oh, there did exist a seedy group of women, whores by any other name, women who loved the power they believed at their command when they seduced a military man; but Julie belonged to a different league: she was the *crème de la crème*, the most sought-after woman on the base. And Julie was beautiful—with curves so shapely they brought tears to the eyes of even the most faithful of husbands. And she was ambitious. It was Julie's way to play one man off another. She would do anything to satisfy the desires of her current beau— and she could!—but always at a price; Julie was always after something. Perhaps one night she had gone too far, asked too much. Or perhaps, as Kincaid suspected, robbery was the motive and Julie had simply been in the wrong place at the wrong time.

"Which of you discovered the body?" the investigator asked.

Kincaid indicated that he had. Though a lie, this was a commendable action on his part; faithful soldier that he was, he did not wish to involve his commanding officer in an interrogation when he could easily supply the details. He gave an account of how he had come across the body and of his whereabouts that night. He told the investigator his theory about robbery and indicated the necklace. "The robber must have heard me coming and panicked," he said. The investigator mumbled something about a lovers' quarrel and turned to the body. And Kincaid turned to O'Neill, but his commanding officer was in no shape to converse: his eyes were staring vacantly at the constellation Orion which hung low in the western sky.

When his preliminary examination of the body was complete, the investigator looked back at Kincaid. "We'll be in touch if we need you," he said.

Kincaid nodded. I'll leave the investigating to the investigators, he thought and then he returned to his barracks. His last view of the murder scene was of two men lifting Julie's body onto a stretcher before they carried it away.

Who were these two men, O'Neill and Kincaid? O'Neill was a giant of a man, with a large head, enormous ears, and thick, muscular legs. He was forty-two years old, married, no children. He was known by everyone—except Kincaid—to have fooled around with the ladies, an activity which caused his wife no small amount of grief. As a commander, O'Neill was said to be strict, yet fair, kind-hearted and humane, one of those people who always seem to be in a good mood. He was well liked by his men, though there were exceptions, and at least one man was known to detest him. Kincaid, on the other hand, was of medium build, average height, nondescript in appearance, mid-twenties, unmarried. If his appearance was ordinary, his personality was even more so. Most people had trouble remembering the slightest aspects of his character. A loner, he kept to himself. It is known that Kincaid admired O'Neill as a commanding officer. O'Neill had authored three books on military life, books Kincaid had studied diligently, underlining salient passages and even going so far as to memorize entire sections which he would repeat word for word to the amazement of the others in his regiment. On several occasions Kincaid is known to have mentioned that O'Neill considered Kincaid destined to become a great soldier, perhaps a member of the top brass, though no one remembers O'Neill ever singling out Kincaid for praise or special commendation.

The next few days brought noticeable changes to the life of Kincaid. The murder affected him profoundly, casting a shadow over every event and action, every thought, word, and deed in his own life. Perhaps it was the sight of Julie's corpse, so hideous to behold, the smell of death in the air. Perhaps—even so—the serenity in her face, the calm in her eyes, which would forever be etched in his mind. Who can say why any event causes us to change and to see the meaning of things in a different light? Suffice it to say that in Kincaid's case this had happened.

A week passed during which one event of extreme importance occurred: Julie Blain's necklace vanished. It had been kept in a safe at police headquarters, but when a member of the investigative team opened the safe one day to examine the jewels, it was nowhere to be seen. With the necklace gone and no fingerprints on the knife, the investigators had nothing on which to build a case. The police had no suspects and seemed resigned to the fact that the crime would never be solved. The case was not closed, but no progress was made: the result was the same.

One Saturday evening after hours of drinking, a group of soldiers from Kincaid's regiment, hoping to relieve the poor man's depression, talked him into visiting a brothel. Kincaid had never gone to such an establishment. Nor was he the type to do so. But drink can make a man do things he would never normally consider.

The whorehouse was labyrinthine—or so it seemed to Kincaid—dozens of musty, dimly-lit corridors with doors on both sides. Kincaid stood around with the others, waiting his turn; when it came he was led to the end of one corridor, a room on the left. He entered and saw a young girl on the bed, her body smelling of lavender, her hair scented with rum. The room was illuminated by a dozen candles which cast flickering shadows on light-green walls. The girl indicated she would do whatever Kincaid desired and, believing she knew what he desired, began unbuttoning her blouse, an enchanting prospect to be sure, but what Kincaid saw next made him recoil in horror; he blinked in disbelief but there was no mistaking it: around the girl's neck was Julie's diamond necklace.

"Those jewels—let me see them!" he stammered, his hands groping outward.

The girl, who was not particularly intelligent, thought Kincaid wanted the necklace as part of some exotic sexual rite—this is what she herself told me—and she unfastened its gold clasp and handed them over. The diamonds gleamed brightly and Kincaid saw that they were indeed the same stones that had graced Julie's neck. "Oh God, no!" he cried. And much to the young lady's astonishment, he dropped the necklace and rushed out of the room.

Later that evening, the soldiers went to Kincaid's quarters intending to ask how he had made out. They were shocked to find him pale and frightened, his eyes trembling with fear. Stuttering horrendously, he told them the woman resembled Julie Blain, that she tried to force herself upon him, and of his abrupt flight. He omitted any mention of the jewels. Much to his surprise, he was greeted with laughter. "That sounds like Peg," somebody said. "She's one of O'Neill's women."

Accounts differ as to what happened next. One source says Kincaid, sitting morbidly in a local bar, claimed he saw the sergeant dancing arm in arm with Julie Blain; another, that Kincaid said it was not Ms. Blain but the devil himself, clothed in red robes of regal splendor. One day Kincaid said he happened upon O'Neill and Ms. Blain kissing in an alleyway; he implored O'Neill to leave the woman alone, but his commander ignored his entreaties, and instead, as Julie uttered an audible moan, pushed her to the ground, crushing his lips against hers, his hand moving beneath her dress. Why Kincaid would begin having these hallucinations is obvious to any student of psychology, but it was not obvious to the authorities: they took this as proof that *Kincaid* was the guilty man. And it is not hard to see how they would have come to such a conclusion.

Rumors spread throughout the base that an arrest was near, though no names were mentioned. Kincaid, believing O'Neill was the one to be arrested, realized his commander must be warned at once.

That night Kincaid went to a military nightclub, The Spot, hoping the entertainment might ease his troubled mind. He dined alone. On stage were members of a traveling burlesque show. Kincaid was watching, trying in vain to enjoy the comedy, when there was sudden commotion at the table behind him. Turning around, he was surprised to see O'Neill rise angrily from his chair and shout at his wife, a petite woman with a freckled complexion, her red hair pulled up in a bun. O'Neill glared at the woman—his face red, the veins bulging on his neck—and then he reached out and slapped her face. At this she burst into tears. Never had Kincaid seen his commanding officer in such a mood.

O'Neill started to leave, but then he wheeled around and cried, "From now on, mind your own business, woman!"

"Sergeant," interjected Kincaid. "The jewels! They know about the jewels!"

O'Neill turned to face Kincaid and for a moment Kincaid thought he saw fear in the sergeant's eyes. But just as quickly it vanished, and he stabbed the air with his forefinger, exclaiming, "Silence! You're drunk, soldier!"

Kincaid opened his mouth to protest—the sergeant must have misunderstood—but his commander was already out the door.

When Kincaid reached O'Neill's office early the next morning, intending to warn his commander once again that he was in jeopardy, the door opened before he could knock—it was as though O'Neill was expecting Kincaid—and the sergeant stood before him, his massive frame made more massive by the violent tendencies Kincaid knew he possessed.

"They're on to you, Sergeant," Kincaid said.

O'Neill, apparently unmoved, simply nodded. "I guess that they are," he replied. "What surprises me is what took them so long."

Kincaid began to wonder if something was terribly wrong. Was it the drone in his commander's voice?

"But they're mad," continued O'Neill.

"Mad?"

"Just as *you* are mad."

Each man stared at the other: O'Neill hypnotically, Kincaid with a look of unease. And when O'Neill finally spoke, breaking the shadowy silence, he droned like a somnambulist: "At the murder scene, I wasn't in shock. I was calculating probabilities, determining the course of events. In a matter of seconds I knew what the future held: I saw into time, I saw into space, I knew what was and what would be." O'Neill paused, for Kincaid had begun to tremble. "Events themselves are of little consequence," he continued, "more important is how we *perceive* events, for that is what governs our actions. In the brothel you saw Julie's necklace, or rather, you saw what you imagined to be Julie's necklace and that vision started your mind on a journey that led you here—which *had* to lead you here. Unfortunately, you erred in one important detail: I didn't kill Julie Blain. *You* did."

I am sure no one amongst you has ever known the terror Kincaid felt. He stiffened and there was horror engraved on his face. O'Neill continued icily:

"To help you atone for your crime I'm now going to shoot you. But first—there's one small thing I'd like you to do."

Minutes later a shot rang out. Kincaid uttered a cry as the bullet shattered his brain and he crumpled to the floor.

* * *

Later that evening the police discovered Kincaid's body stretched out on the ground near to where Julie Blain had met her tragic end. One hand held a gun, the other was arranged neatly over his chest. A suicide note, dictated by O'Neill, written and signed by Kincaid, revealed Kincaid's final moments of agony and despair. It concluded: "I can't live any longer with the blood of Julie on my hands. I killed her, she whom I loved."

The investigator, relieved that the case had reached its conclusion, removed the gun from the dead man's hand and twirled it about his fingers. He turned to the chief of police and smiled.

RHONDA'S STORY

It was four years ago, in the fall of 1892, when my father, Ricky Treyburn, was charged with the murder of a prostitute in Corpus Christi where we lived. The woman had been raped and strangled, her body set aflame. While in prison awaiting trial, my father maintained a stony silence, even when the sheriff found evidence connecting him to the deaths of three other women. Two of the latter crimes were unsolved, but as for the third, another man, a Mr. Randolph Rice, had been convicted and was serving time in prison. Mr. Rice had always maintained his innocence.

During the trial, the testimony of each witness for the prosecution was like a nail in my father's coffin. My father, it was said, was a member of the notorious Red Jack Gang, a gang that preyed on stagecoaches that ran through central Texas. He was a cattle rustler and racketeer. And the head of a prostitution ring. Mr. Alasso—an ugly man with enormous hands and a pale, wolf-like face—was the most damaging witness. After receiving immunity from prosecution, he testified that he had helped my father establish a bordello in Houston. He spoke of my father's wild temper and fits of drunkenness. Mr. Alasso claimed that on more than one occasion he heard my father threaten the girls, and once came upon him beating a sixteen-year-old runaway whom he had recently hired.

My father looked at the floor and occasionally glanced up at the jury. A quiet, unassuming man, he hardly seemed the portrait of evil who was painstakingly being depicted.

The defense said that the prosecution's case was character assassination, pure and simple, that it had nothing to do with the charges against my father. It was pointed out that no one was able to connect my father to the murdered women. There were no fingerprints, no murder weapons, not even a motive had been put forward.

But the arguments failed to sway the jury, who deliberated less than a day before returning the guilty verdict. My father was sentenced to hang.

He showed no emotion when the verdict was read. When asked if he wished to make a statement, he spoke seven words: "Your Honor, I wasn't part of it." The judge stared at him and asked if that was all he had to say. He was silent. A deputy led him away. I never saw him again. The entire trial, through the jury's empanelment, to the steady parade of witnesses, to the sad and weighty conclusion, took two weeks. Mr. Rice was released from prison, and sentence was carried out the next day.

My mother did not miss a moment of my father's trial. Throughout the proceedings, she sat behind him, her hands folded in her lap, her long chestnut-brown hair, which she normally wore loose, pulled up in a bun. A kind and gentle woman, she radiated peace in a courtroom clamoring for my father's blood.

"He didn't do it, Rhonda," she said after the trial ended. "He wasn't capable."

"But why was he silent?"

"I don't know."

With my father dead, the health of my mother deteriorated rapidly. They had been married thirty years and were as devoted to each other as any couple had ever been.

Even though my father had been found guilty in a court of law, my mother was convinced of his innocence.

And equally convinced that one day his name would be cleared.

"He was framed," she told me, repeating the sentence again and again.

That winter my mother caught pneumonia, and after six weeks, died in her sleep one December evening. It was a dismal night I'll never forget. I cried for what seemed like an eternity.

I had an older brother who lived in San Francisco. Ted Treyburn. Twenty-eight years old. Ten years older than me.

Not only had my brother not attended the trial, but we had not heard from him the entire time. It was not unexpected. My brother had been estranged from the family for years, having quarreled with my father shortly before leaving home, insisting he would never set foot in Corpus Christi again. I never learned the reason for their argument. I am not sure anyone knew the reason for their argument. Here today—writing these words in a cold prison cell that may as well be my coffin—I still do not know if there *was* an argument.

It was upon the death of my mother that my brother returned from California. One look told me something was wrong. A coolness that bordered on arrogance. Our parents were dead, for God's sake, but Ted attended my mother's funeral displaying an attitude of chilling indifference. Unfortunately, I was too overcome with grief to make inquiries into my brother's state of mind.

Ted was staying with his wife at a hotel in town, and the evening before he was to return to San Francisco I went to see him. I went to say good-bye. That was all I intended to do.

Ted was not there, but his wife was. I had never met her—she had taken ill the night before the funeral, my brother had said, and sent her condolences—and when the door opened I saw before me a beautiful blonde in her early twenties, her hair a waterfall of curls. She was wearing a white pleated floor-length skirt and a lace pastel blouse with ruffled sleeves. Her eyes were light green, her arms long and slender, her fingernails exquisite. She introduced herself as Donna and invited me inside. Ted would be back shortly, she said, and surely would love to see me. I stepped inside and she shut the door. I found myself in a lavish suite. It was hardly what I expected for I had never thought of my brother as particularly well-off. Donna told me to have a seat on the couch and went to fix drinks at a bar adjoining the kitchen. I looked around the room. Two opened suitcases on the floor. A pile of dirty clothes near the window. A newspaper on an end table next to the couch. An ashtray filled with cigarette butts. I went over to the couch and sat down. I happened to glance over the armrest and saw dozens of albumen prints scattered on the floor. I picked up one and examined it. A crude image of a lady of the evening in provocative dress, her breasts exposed. To say I felt ill would have been an understatement.

Donna returned with my drink and saw me looking at the photograph. She did not act surprised. She said:

"Ted's told me much about you. I'm glad we had a chance to meet before we return to Chicago."

My spine stiffened. "I thought you lived in San Francisco," I said.

She frowned. "Where did you get that idea?"

"It's what Ted told us." I turned the photograph over. I put it on the couch. I did not want to be seen holding the photograph.

"You must be confused," she continued. "I've never been in California."

"Mrs. Treyburn—"

"Miss Cox."

"There must be some misunderstanding. My brother, Ted Treyburn, is married." I was not sure what the misunderstanding was and I was not sure I wanted to know. Right then, I just wanted to leave. But before I had a chance to excuse myself, Donna said:

"I'm Ted's girlfriend, Donna Cox. And there's no wife, if that's what you're thinking, though Ted and I have been together for years."

"Excuse me," I said. "But that's not what my brother led us to believe."

"Whatever."

For some reason, I felt emboldened. Maybe it was anger at my brother's betrayal. Or my budding suspicions. Or something else. I don't know. I held up the photograph and said, "What's this?"

The blue-eyed blonde who claimed to be my brother's girlfriend and who was more likely a highly paid prostitute was unfazed. "We brought some prints for the distributor to examine."

"The distributor? You mean you peddle this filth?"

My accusation must have taken her by surprise, for a startled look came over her face. But before she could answer, the door opened and my brother strode into the room. He looked at me and at the photograph beside me. Then he looked at Donna, who was as pale as a ghost. "How'd she get in here?" he said, thrusting a thumb in my direction.

"I'm sorry, Ted," Donna said. "I thought the woman knew."

Ted pulled a revolver from his pocket and pointed it at me—his sister. I inhaled sharply. "Turn around," he said.

"I don't know what's going on," I said, looking into my brother's eyes. "There must be some mistake."

"That's what it looks like."

As I said, something was dreadfully wrong and I had to think fast. I crumpled to the floor in a mock-faint. Lady Luck must have been smiling on me that day, for they were taken in. "She was always weak at heart," my brother crooned. "Such a sissy."

Donna laughed.

My brother said, "You idiot."

"I didn't know, for Christ's sake."

"When are you going to learn to keep your mouth shut?"

"Take it easy. She doesn't know anything."

"She knows plenty. But it doesn't matter what she knows because we're going to get rid of her."

I heard a gasp. Then Donna said, "Ted, you're talking about your sister."

"It's her or me. Now shut up and listen."

"Teddy . . ." I imagined her pouting.

"Don't get sweet with me, babe."

A pause. A sigh. A bitter voice, "Why not? Everyone else does."

The gun went off and I heard a body fall to the floor. Then:

"Oh, my God."

Through the slits of my eyes, I saw my brother next to the door. His face registered shock. He lay the gun on the desk and limped across the room, kneeling where Donna had fallen. "Why did you make me do it, babe?" he sobbed. Then he started to cry. "No, baby, no." No, not a prostitute. Maybe she really was his girlfriend.

Ted's back was to me now and he must have been no more than twenty feet away. I saw the gun on the desk. Smoking still. I inched forward. If he turned around, I was dead. There would be no second chance. At one point my foot knocked against the end table and it made a creaking noise. I stopped short. Every nerve in my body was taut. Luckily, Ted was still spilling tears over the body of his dead girlfriend and he didn't hear. I sighed in relief. Two more feet to go.

And then my brother began to talk. He spoke to himself, but seemed to address his words to someone else, Donna at first, and then a distant other, a higher being perhaps. Moments later I heard what sounded like a window opening. I thought nothing of it at the time. I was mesmerized by the sound of Ted's voice.

He told Donna that he loved her. He told her he did not mean for it to end this way. He told her he was nothing without her. He wanted to die. She had done it.

His kindred spirit. That is what he said. She had done it. She made him do it. And now his life was a void, empty and without meaning. He would go to another place. A place where he could dream in peace.

As my brother blathered on, I noticed that a window in the back of the room was wide open, a gentle breeze rustling the curtains. And that is not all I saw. While Ted hung over the body of Donna, I saw, in the shadows of the room, the figure of my father looking at me. He was wearing a brown vest, jeans, and black boots. His favorite Stetson clutched in his left hand. His pale-blue eyes were filled with despair. And they were urging me to avenge his death.

When I reached the desk, I raised myself to my knees and picked up the gun. I could only pray that there were bullets left in the chamber. I could have retraced my steps to the door, retreated into the hallway and fled down the stairs, but I could not bring myself to do so. At that moment, I was overcome with a feeling of revenge. And of rage. There was only me and Ted in the world. And this piece of warm metal I held in my hands. I did not know exactly what had happened, but I knew enough. *They framed him.* My mother's words came back to me, echoing inside the spaces of my skull. *They framed him, Rhonda.* I heard the voices of my mother and my father. I saw them in my mind's eye. We would never be together. We would never be together because my brother had murdered my father. In cold blood and without remorse. I rose to my feet, aimed the gun, and fired. A single shot. He slumped to the floor and lay still. I pressed the trigger again but nothing happened; the gun was empty. I went to where my brother lay. His blood flowed lazily from a wound in his back. Donna was not two feet away, her eyes staring up at me cold and lifeless, scarlet rivulets of blood on her forehead. I took out my handkerchief and wiped the gun clean. Then I put the gun in her hands. A murder-suicide. The sheriff would never question the death of two outlaws far from home.

I went downstairs. The lobby was empty. I became aware of the pounding of my heart. Of my clammy skin. The shortness of my breath. And of a deathly chill that had overtaken me.

I emerged from the hotel into a drizzly night. I went home, took a shower, and went to bed.

The next morning the town was abuzz with news of the murder-suicide. Yes, the news had come off just as I had hoped. But what followed was worse than I thought possible. The investigation into my brother's death revealed that he had been part of a crime ring headquartered in Chicago, a ring that had recently expanded into the deep south and was in direct competition with my father's.

I was in shock; the world I'd fervently believed in crashed down upon me. Evidently the family's criminal activity was not only beyond dispute but was greater than previously thought. It had—in fact—encompassed the entire mid-section of the country! As you can imagine, the news became the talk of the town and I became something of a celebrity. The questions were endless. How did it feel knowing I had spent my entire life with criminals? Had I suspected what was happening around me? And if not . . .

I tried to be accommodating, but I could only go on for so long. One day I put a halt to it all. I needed to be alone, I said. I would take no more questions. I hid in the house and went out only in the dead of night. I dressed up as a glamorous young woman and fled to a saloon where I drowned my sorrows in drink and deflected amorous glances from men who wanted to help me forget my troubles.

It started as rumors. Rumors that quickly turned hateful. I was a common prostitute and had been involved with my family's criminal activity. Just look at the gaudy clothes I wore. The way I conducted my life. Did I seem like a woman coming to terms with grief?

A different story was put forth. My brother—people said—had left Corpus Christi to escape a life of crime. He took a train to Chicago where he fell in love with Donna. They settled down in the windy city to begin a new life. He was returning to Texas only because he thought it was now safe to do so. But he did not know that I knew of his past. That I blamed him for my parents' deaths.

And then a witness stepped forward. A middle-aged woman who'd been walking past Ted's room when the confrontation occurred. Her ear pressed to the door after the fatal gunshot rang out, she'd heard the words of a dying man who pledged eternal love to his dead girlfriend. Donna's name was spoken. And so was mine. "She did it. My kindred spirit." Clearly a reference to the sister. To Rhonda Treyburn. And then a man came forward and said he had seen me leaving my brother's hotel on that fateful evening. And that was all the evidence that was needed. The story became: I killed Donna Cox, my brother's girlfriend. I allowed my brother a few words of repentance. And then I shot him. In cold blood and with no remorse.

"It wasn't like that," I sobbed.

The whispers became a crescendo that throbbed in my ears. I would have left town, but I knew that if I tried to go I would have been lynched on the spot. And so I did not try. Corpus Christi became my prison.

Surprisingly, the sheriff never questioned me. I knew I was his prime suspect. Indeed, the whole town thought it was me. I guess they wanted to draw out their investigation, wait for me to break down and confess.

One day, after two months of this hell, I could stand the strain no longer. I could not deny that I had been born into a family of outlaws. And it looked as though I must atone for their sins. I went to the sheriff's department. I spoke to a pleasant-looking gentleman with hair graying around his temples. He smiled when I entered the front office, he seemed to be expecting me. He picked up his pen and pulled a blank piece of paper from a drawer. And even before I opened my mouth, he was writing my name with a flourish.

"I did it," I said. "It was me."

My trial was conducted with almost textbook precision and I watched the proceedings with stony detachment. Though urged to do so by my lawyer, I refused to speak on my behalf. Even so, he put up a valiant defense, claiming I murdered in self-defense, but it was all for naught. The townspeople demanded I be punished and I was hardly surprised when a guilty verdict was announced. I expected to be led to the gallows, but my lawyer was able to persuade the judge that leniency was called for. I was given a life sentence.

* * *

The jailer comes mid-morning. I hear the clop-clop of boots as he saunters down the hall, a ring of keys jangling. He really is a nice fellow. There's always a sparkle in his eye. He stays with me sometimes—he outside my cell, looking in—and talks about the world. And even though the world does not interest me, I listen. I listen for he interests me. Life is a series of forks on the trail, he tells me. You take one branch and then you move on. I smile. I know exactly what he means.

OTHERS

I love Elaine, but I love Katrina incomparably more. There are no secrets between Elaine and me, there is only love, a love that has grown stronger with the passage of time, through our courtship, marriage, the raising of our children. But that is not the issue. It is not a question regarding love; it is a statement of fact regarding the degree of love. I love Elaine—I shall always love Elaine—but it is Katrina whom I worship, whom I wish to hold in my arms, whose lips I wish to kiss. We are like two threads wrapped around an invisible core, Katrina and I: one cannot see what binds us, but we are, inexplicably, bound.

I came upon Katrina on a Sunday afternoon when Elaine brought her portrait home from the auction. I watched in silence as Elaine placed it on the mantle above our fireplace and dusted off the frame. The picture—it was a sixteenth-century oil painting—portrayed a beautiful young woman wearing a white dress that fell to her ankles. Katrina—this is the name I have given her; her true name has been lost in the annals of history—was facing the viewer but seemed to be looking past him into the distance. She had large, brown eyes; a white complexion; broad, high cheekbones; dark hair that fell to her shoulders. Her lips were pressed tightly together as if in apprehension or in fear, which served only to highlight her features.

I must have lost myself in this image of forgotten beauty, for when I came to my wife was gone. I drew near the painting and swept my fingers across the canvas, touching Katrina's eyes, her face and lips. In the bottom right corner I noticed a signature scratched across the surface of the canvas; it was barely legible and I had to look closely to make it out: 'Klaus Van Klaus' I read. I did not recognize the name.

That evening I asked Elaine about the picture; she told me she had never heard of a 'Klaus Van Klaus,' had bought the painting simply because she thought it a splendid example of sixteenth-century portraiture—and because it was dark and would not show the soot from the fireplace.

"And the woman?"

"Who is she? Who knows? A friend of the painter, perhaps, or the wife of an Italian nobleman. She has a captivating look about her, doesn't she?"

I returned to the painting often over the next several weeks: every morning before leaving for work and again before going to bed. To say I was haunted by the picture would have been an understatement. Indeed, I had never seen such a beautiful woman; through her Van Klaus had captured the very essence of Beauty on his canvas. What a remarkable painter he must have been! And Katrina, who had she been and what had become of her? Her sad, wistful eyes revealed the solitude that seemed to fill her soul.

Can one fall in love with a portrait, with an image? Truly, truly fall in love? This is the question I asked myself. I felt that sinking feeling of incipient love descend upon me as I gazed at Katrina, a feeling I had felt only once before, with Elaine, when she entered my life. I love Elaine, but I love Katrina . . . She is dead, Rathskeller, I told myself. But I could not make myself believe it. And when I looked at her portrait—it was so life-like, so real— it seemed to me that she, Katrina, was real. As real as I. What, then, was I to do? I found myself unable to pass her portrait without losing myself in wonder and reflection. Yet I could not insult Elaine by suggesting she return the picture. What reason would I give? That I had fallen in love with the woman in the painting? But neither could I continue to endure Katrina's endless stares, her penetrating gaze, her thoughts that controlled my thoughts. I could no longer sleep at night. I tossed and turned like a ship that is lost at sea.

"Is something the matter?" Elaine asked one evening, as she kissed me before turning out the light. No, I said. Did she think something was wrong? She told me my kisses seemed distant. I smiled. It was only her imagination, I said. I leaned over and brushed her cheek.

Was I to tell her my kisses were meant for someone more remote, a pale image of pigment and light? But the more I pondered, the more I wondered: were we really so far apart, Katrina and I? She was an image in my world and I was an image in hers and so we were both images of the world. There was no fundamental difference between us. I hoped that somehow this knowledge might make my situation easier, that I could live knowing that across the bounds of time and space Katrina and I had met.

Things went from bad to worse. Try as I might I simply could not stop thinking about Katrina. I no longer responded to my children when they addressed me (I was listening only for Katrina's voice, Katrina's words); I ignored my wife; I sulked; I became forgetful; one day my supervisor caught me napping at work, he said I looked tired and distressed; what was I to tell him? (I said nothing.) And then one night my dreams turned into nightmares. I imagined the construction of a wall rising slowly brick by brick between Katrina and I, and I stared into the bricklayer's leaden eyes and cried out in dismay when I could no longer see Katrina, could no longer hear her siren's voice. I broke down and wept. All was darkness when I woke and realized I was alone, that Katrina was dead and buried, that I would never hold her in my arms. Elaine was asleep beside me, but I was alone: alone with my thoughts of a dead woman whom I loved.

You are a fool, you are an idiot, I thought to myself. Get control of yourself, for God's sake, Rathskeller. Elaine looked so peaceful as she slept, but who knew what she might have been dreaming of: a love that had been lost, a cunning deception, the burning fever in a troubled husband's heart. . . .

You cannot go on living like this, I told myself. Not a day longer. And so, to alleviate the discord in my heart and attempt to restore the harmony of our family, I set out later that day for the town library, intending to learn all I could about Klaus Van Klaus and his mysterious and beautiful subject. Perhaps learning more about Katrina would make her seem more ordinary, less mysterious, and would put to rest my wild flights of fancy.

The reference librarian directed me to the six-volume Encyclopedia of Painters and Portraits, the 53d edition; the definitive work on the subject, she said. I was certain to find my painter there. I looked at Volume I and saw that the painters were arranged chronologically and then by country. Excitedly, I turned to the index, which I found at the end of Volume VI. There, among the Van Gogh's and the Van Allen's and the Van Rosse's, I found Van Klaus—pages 1016-1030, Volume V. But my excitement turned to despair for on none of those pages did I see any mention of a 'Klaus Van Klaus.' The only entry was for the sixteenth-century Gothic painter Abdul de Vassis.

Perhaps a different volume? I looked at the same pages in the other five volumes (each volume contained roughly 2000 pages) but saw no mention of Van Klaus. I went back to the librarian and pointed out the discrepancy.

"That's strange," she said.

The card catalogs listed two earlier editions of the book which the library owned. "Perhaps that entry was dropped from the current edition," she said. She led me to the downstairs stacks. There I found the Encyclopedia of Painters and Portraits the 52nd edition. I turned to the index and saw Klaus Van Klaus's name as before. Pages

1016-1030. If only I could have found them—but pages 1016-1030 were missing from the volume! I saw no evidence the book had been tampered with; the pages simply were not there. I looked at the librarian in dismay, but she was not alarmed:

"Most likely this painter was removed from the Encyclopedia beginning with the 52nd edition," she said. "Probably a last-minute decision, thus the misnumbered pages; moreover, they forgot to remove his name from the index. The page numbering was corrected with the last edition, although his name is still in the index."

"Of course," I said, though I wasn't convinced. "The other edition? You said there were two others."

"Yes. The Rare Book Room. It's not the edition previous to this one, which would have been the 51st edition; it's an original edition—the 1st Edition. Perhaps you'll find your painter there."

We wove down aisle after aisle and finally reached a room with no windows and a padlocked wooden door.

"In here," she said.

She opened the door and led me inside. The air was so musty that I could hardly breathe. She switched on a light, then disappeared into the back of the room, returning with a dusty, misshaped tome, a five-volume work, printed over one hundred years before. The Encyclopedia of Painters and Portraits, Edition I, stamped on the spine.

"Wonderful," I said as she put the volumes into my outstretched hands. Klaus Van Klaus, pages 864-878, Volume V. And this time I found what I was searching for: there before my eyes were fifteen pages devoted to my beloved painter. I learned that Van Klaus had been a minor nineteenth century German painter, that he had been fond of painting the wives of German nobleman, that he had a torrid love affair with one of them, that he was challenged to a duel by the lady's husband, Count LaMore VI, that Van Klaus killed the Count with a rapier thrust through the heart, that he fled on foot into the Black Forest of Germany, that he reappeared several years later, disguised as a mendicant, offering to paint portraits for lodging and food, that he confronted his former lover one evening as she left her residence on her sister's arm, that she refused to look at him, that he grew incensed, raved like a lunatic, threatened to kill both her and her sister, and that when she threatened to call the police, had disappeared into the night and was never seen or heard of again. Finally, and most importantly, I learned that none of Van Klaus's paintings were known to have survived to the present day.

I closed the book, leaned back in my chair, and sighed. My trip to the library had raised more questions than it had answered: Who was Klaus Van Klaus? I did not know. Who was the woman in the painting? I did not know. And why was Van Klaus destined to disappear from history at the same time the woman was to reappear, with myself to bear witness to her second coming? I did not know. But I could not deny the fact that it had happened. Even now it was unfolding. Look at me covered with dust, look how Katrina directed my life!

I switched off the light and turned to go.

And then, like a dream descending, I saw Katrina before me, her eyes like sapphires, glowing in the dark. She beckoned me to her, and I approached. "Katrina!" I said. "Katrina, Katrina, Katrina! My darling Katrina! It's me, it's Rathskeller!" I kissed her on the face and neck and she returned my kisses, her mouth moist, her face flushed with passion. And then, just as suddenly, she grew cold; the vision faded, and I cried out in despair as I realized she was gone.

When I reached home, Elaine met me at the door. "You look pale," she said. I shrugged. What was I to tell her? I went into the kitchen to get myself a drink. There I saw my two daughters playing cards at the breakfast table. I looked at them and forced a smile. "Hi dad," Jean mumbled. Then added, "Is something wrong?" I shook my head, no. I was tired, I said. I shut the refrigerator door and went into the living room, collapsing onto the couch. My head was splitting. I set my drink down on the end table; moments later I was asleep.

I awoke to silence. My head no longer ached. Someone had put a blanket over me. Elaine, no doubt. I smiled. For the first time in weeks I felt content.

My eyes wandered about the room and settled over the fireplace. It was then I received what was to be the first of several shocks that evening: the picture of Katrina was gone, replaced by a picture of children at a carnival, a picture full of bright colors and smiling faces. I looked frantically about the room for Katrina but did not see her. I did, however, see Elaine as she crossed the portal from the dining room, drew near me and, smiling, kissed my forehead.

"It's in the basement, dear," she said. "I'll take it to the dealer in the morning."

I didn't acknowledge her, but instead hurried downstairs, like a man possessed by fear, my happiness having vanished in that instant. There I saw, to my immense relief, Van Klaus's picture atop an old bookshelf next to the furnace. Katrina, my Katrina.

Only it was not Katrina. Or, rather, it was Katrina, another Katrina, Katrina and her beloved holding each other in a matrimonial embrace. "Katrina?" The word escaped my lips. She, being an image on canvas, did not respond. She was dressed in black as was her lover; their figures blended into the background of the painting so that you could make out only their faces; two faces starstruck and filled with beauty: Katrina's lover was quite handsome, his face serene, his eyes blue and radiating love. Her face was more beautiful than ever, white as alabaster, smooth as any pearl. Katrina, the betrothed. Katrina, Katrina, Katrina. I know what you are thinking. And, of course, any fool would have questioned the validity of what I was seeing. But I was dealing with the supernatural—of this I was convinced—something beyond reality, something strange . . . and wonderful.

That night I could not sleep. My thoughts twisted themselves into Gordian knots, holding me prisoner to unearthly imaginings. At one point, I reached over and touched Elaine, thinking it was Katrina, but she drew away. I took her hand in mine; I tried to calm my nerves. I went to the window and stared into the tenebrous night. The sky was pitch-black; there was no moon, no stars to calm me. I went into the kitchen and poured myself a drink. It was then I thought I heard a woman's voice softly calling my name, calling from beneath the floorboards. I put down my drink and, drawing my bathrobe tightly about me, descended the basement stairs. I did not turn on the light, I did not call out to the voice I had heard, I did not wish to disturb what might lie in the darkness below. I had to determine in shadowy silence and by my own observation what was happening. Had Katrina metamorphosed yet again: Katrina as Mother with Child? Or had she vanished from the face of the earth and the voice I heard was the voice of her ghost, calling out to me? Or perhaps she was as she first had been: Katrina the Alluring. Katrina the Bewitching. But when I reached the bottom of the stairs, drew near the furnace in the darkness, reached out and took up the painting in my hands, the image that met my eyes was more disturbing than I ever could have imagined: there was Katrina, alone in the picture as before—only this time her hair was pulled up in a bun, revealing a long, graceful neck; her eyes looked like two emeralds, glowing brightly like a cat's eyes in the night; her lips were open as if beckoning the viewer in a kiss and—this, the most alarming—her blouse was unbuttoned, revealing her breasts. Katrina the Vixen. Katrina the Whore. And then I saw her, I saw Katrina—and I swear that this is true— as she opened her lips and called out my name. I staggered back in disbelief—was I going mad?—I collapsed onto the floor, sobbing uncontrollably, my head in my hands.

And that is how Elaine found me at dawn. She led me to our bedroom; she looked tired and confused. I was trembling like a child, my mind lost in a fog of delirium. I heard her say she'd found me clutching the painting to my chest and calling out a woman's name. Certainly she suspected infidelity—what else could she have thought?—and perhaps love of the supernatural is infidelity of a sort.

I awoke that day around noon. The house was empty. A note in the kitchen, from Elaine, said she had taken the kids for the day, that she hoped I was feeling better, and that leftovers from last night's dinner were in the freezer. I knew what I had to do; I was no longer afraid. I descended the steps into the basement. There I found the portrait of Katrina in the armchair, just where Elaine had placed it, just where I had come upon it. Katrina was as I had first seen her; perhaps as she had always been, as Klaus Van Klaus had painted her. I picked up the painting and went outside. I got into our car, backed it out the driveway, and started down the street.

There is something about height. Something vast, majestic—and alluring. Perhaps it is because from the heights one can see all that lies below, one can put things in perspective. Perhaps that from the heights the air is more rarefied and pure and that one can think more clearly. Or perhaps it is something more mysterious, more ethereal: perhaps that from the heights one is closer to the mind of God. And it was the heights I was now seeking: a place called Bald Mountain, a two-hour drive from our town. Bald Mountain is the strangest looking mountain I have ever seen, green with vegetation at the bottom, rising sharply—a sixty-degree angle—to a huge granite peak. The top had been decimated by a blight in the early twentieth century, hence the mountain's name. A road—Bald Mountain Drive—wound round and round the mountain to the top. I had taken it several times before, always, it seemed, during times of crisis. A family of buzzards lived near the peak, large, crafty-looking birds, who hung upside down from dead tree limbs and gazed uneasily at anyone who dared invade their territory. I scowled at them as I passed by.

The sky was matted with thick low clouds that hung over me and seemed to oppress my mind. When I reached a clearing, I built a fire from sticks I'd gathered at the top of the mountain. The wood was tinder-dry—it hadn't rained in weeks—and soon the fire was roaring. The buzzards looked at it—and at me—warily but did not move. I felt a cool breeze against my skin. I would make of myself and Katrina our own portrait: 'Rathskeller and the Maiden.' With a final kiss and a sigh I threw the picture in. The fire died down for a moment, as if sizing up this new addition, then picked up again as the wooden frame began to burn. By a peculiar twist of fate the picture landed upright so that Katrina was visible. Her eyes cold and lifeless, her body rigid, I found it hard to imagine I had ever thought her otherwise. The fire erupted in flame as the canvas exploded into a myriad of colors: orange, white, pink, blue, and the deepest, darkest red.

Katrina, like Van Klaus, was no more. As far as the world was concerned, she never had been. She existed only in my mind and with time that image, too, would fade and my life, though incomparably duller, would be livable once again.

I sighed. I looked up at the sky, at the dead trees that surrounded me, at the vultures who didn't know what to make of me. I put out the fire. I got into my car and drove away.

A MATTER OF PRINCIPLE

I'm not sure I follow you, Charles," I said. "I hear your words, but I don't fully grasp their meaning. This issue of moral relativism—do you really mean to say that nothing is inherently good or evil?"

"That is exactly what I mean," he replied. "And note your use of the word 'inherently'. Consider the case of the wife who poisons her husband. You might think that a clear-cut evil deed. What if I told you the husband beat his wife until she was black and blue and that he threatened to kill her if she contacted the police?"

"That is no excuse for murder."

"Perhaps you would feel better if she killed him quickly. A single bullet through the skull while he slept?"

"But—"

"But nothing. She feared for her life. She was a prisoner in her home. She couldn't contact anyone. She had a right to self-defense."

"She did, but even so her deed was evil."

"I say it was not."

I sighed. "Look," I said exasperatedly. "If you're saying things aren't always what they appear to be, I couldn't agree with you more. But if you mean to imply that a murderer can justify the most heinous of crimes—that is a claim I cannot accept."

He smiled and I realized I had fallen into a trap. He took a sip from a cup of Turkish coffee I had prepared for him at his request and smacked his lips. I had built a fire as I waited for him to arrive that evening and I watched as he stared vacantly into the flames. It was bitterly cold outside and a harsh wind was blowing, the limbs of a pine tree knocking ominously against the gutters. The winters in Pittsburgh were often brutal.

He opened a briefcase and pulled from it a manuscript. "Consider this story," he began. "I believe it illustrates my point. I was eight years old when these events occurred and I know them to be true. My father repeated the incident in detail when I was older and I wrote it down. Even though time has fogged my mind, I remember it as if it were yesterday."

I

Jason Lewd [Charles read] was a loner. He lived in a two-bedroom house on a cul-de-sac in a middle-class neighborhood in Pittsburgh. Jason was thirty-seven years old, tall and stocky, with light-brown hair and blue eyes. He was married but had no children.

For the past several years he had worked as a postal clerk in the downtown branch. He was a hard-working employee and always received favorable reviews. Even so, he associated with his co-workers only when necessary and was considered by most to be arrogant.

For his part, Jason complained to his wife that the other employees were crude in nature. Their talk disgusted him, he said, as well as the never-ending stream of tasteless jokes that were invariably of a sexual nature.

Jason's wife was named Marie. She was seven years his junior. A petite woman with shoulder-length red hair, green eyes, and a beautiful complexion, she was—to put it plainly—a real beauty. Marie was an elementary school teacher at Creekside Elementary in the Pittsburgh Public School system. She usually taught third grade though this year had taken over a fourth-grade classroom to fill in for a teacher who was out on maternity leave.

Creekside was one of the older, more established schools in Pittsburgh. It was a large two-story brick building in the middle of town that taught over eight hundred students. The principal, Sue Templeton, was well-liked and had been there twenty-five years, first as a teacher before moving into administration. It was Sue who recruited Marie from a county school years before. She recalled the pride she had felt when Marie won Teacher of the Year honors in only her second year at Creekside.

There was a sixth-grade teacher at Creekside named Rob Sullivan. Rob was new to the district. He was thirty-three years old, six feet two, with jet-black hair, thick arms and legs. His voice was a soothing baritone that echoed throughout the classroom. Rob was unmarried and had a crush on Marie. He was open about his interest in the young schoolteacher, but always in a friendly, bantering way and she thought nothing about it.

"How is the charming Mrs. Lewd today," he would say or, "Marie, you look lovely this morning," or, if he was feeling particularly bold, "You look positively smashing in red!"

Marie flirted with Rob as well, though she was only joking. Even so, she was not as cautious as she should have been. Gossip spread like wildfire at Creekside.

"I'm feeling fine," she would reply with a smile or, "It's nice to be noticed," or, if she was feeling particularly flirtatious, "You are an alluring man!"

Rob was merely being friendly, Marie felt, but her husband thought otherwise.

"Come now, Jason," she said one evening after dinner. "Rob is harmless."

"I hardly think a man who sends a married woman love poems is harmless," her husband replied with a frown.

"I think they're rather good. Especially the one where he compares me to a summer's day."

Jason scowled. "They sound like they were written by one of your students."

"Jason—you're jealous!" She took his hand. "Please don't worry."

If only Jason wouldn't worry. But that wasn't his nature. And besides, he knew what men would do for romance. He was surrounded by such men all day.

When the school year ended, Marie announced she would not be returning. She gave no explanation. She had been teaching at Creekside for eight years and would be dearly missed, the principal said. Was there anything they could do?

Marie shook her head, no. It was purely a personal matter.

"Are you certain?"

"Yes."

"Perhaps a leave of absence? This would give you the option of returning—"

"No, please. My decision is final."

* * *

That summer was the hottest on record in Pittsburgh. The temperature reached 104 degrees on numerous occasions and the humidity was stifling. One evening there was a ferocious storm with hundreds of lightning strikes. Wildfires erupted on the outskirts of the city, lasting for hours before eventually burning out.

When September came things returned to normal. Creekside opened without Marie. Her classroom was taken over by a recent graduate from the University of Pittsburgh, a young woman with long blond hair and starry eyes.

Rob missed Marie dreadfully. At first he was haunted by the thought that she had left because of him. He had meant only to engage in playful banter, but perhaps he had gone too far. On further reflection he realized the idea was preposterous. Each knew and respected the bounds of their relationship. There was no point in torturing himself over what he knew—deep-down—was a wild improbability.

One day in late September he decided to go over to Marie's house and let her know how things were going at school. She hadn't asked to be kept informed, which he always thought odd, but surely she would appreciate a visit. He couldn't imagine her simply staying home and doing—what?

To be honest, Rob felt uneasy about the way in which Marie had left. In the weeks before she resigned she hadn't been herself; she was moody and seemed depressed. He was reluctant to ask if something was wrong. She'd never talked about her life outside of school. Only that she was married and had no children. Perhaps something else going on. Something unspoken.

Before Rob went to see Marie he decided to find out what he could about her husband. He'd heard rumors about Jason's reclusive nature—he'd never even been to Creekside as far as Rob knew. And that was when he got concerned.

The men he talked to at the post office were less than complimentary about Jason. According to them he was surly, short-tempered, uncivil, and gruff. He rebuffed any attempt to be engaged in conversation. Numerous times he seemed about to explode in anger, usually over the most trivial matters. Once he got into an argument with someone on the phone, a conversation that left him red-faced with rage. It turned out that only the month before—three months after Marie left—Jason had turned in his resignation. Everyone had been quite relieved on that day.

"No, I don't mind talking to you about him now that he's left," Jason's boss said. "He was a hard worker, but a real weirdo. I asked him once about his family. Boy, was that a mistake! He glared at me as if to say: 'Mind your own business.' But of course he said nothing.

He rarely spoke at all. I had the feeling he harbored some dark secret. Something that hurt to talk about."

The Lewds lived in a white two-story house on a tree-lined street in Squirrel Hill. There were two silver elm trees in the front yard and rhododendron bushes with lavender blossoms. Out back a flower garden that contained red and yellow roses, daffodils, zinnias, and a variety of herbs. Jason's neighbors echoed his co-workers' opinion. He never said hello, would merely shrug if spoken to. Marie worked in the yard most evenings and loved to engage in conversation with passersby. When asked about her husband, however, she said little more than: "He's busy at work."

Rob suspected Marie left Creekside because something had happened between her and her husband. There was something she let slip once: Sometimes the people you think you know best you really know the least. She had been talking about a former friend but—was it the wistful look in her eyes?—Rob had the feeling she was referring to someone much closer.

So it was with great trepidation that he walked up the steps to the front door of the Lewd residence and pressed the doorbell. The door swung open, creaking like a coffin lid, and a man poked his head out. He looked to be in his late thirties, had curly light-brown hair, blue eyes, bushy eyebrows.

"Yes?"

Rob explained the purpose of his visit.

"You that Rob fellow?"

"Yep."

The man smiled. "Come in."

II

The preceding events occurred on a Friday evening. Rob's disappearance wasn't noticed until Monday morning when he didn't report to work. Rob was a responsible employee and always called in to report an absence, so an unexplained absence was cause for concern. The front office called his home but got no answer. They did nothing further that day, but when Rob did not show the next morning they called the police.

* * *

The police department's preliminary investigation turned up nothing unusual in Rob's past. Another teacher mentioned that Rob seemed troubled by Marie's departure. It was clear to the police that Rob and Marie had had a close working relationship. Jason's misanthropic ways were also uncovered.

The police theorized there may have been a domestic dispute. Officers were dispatched to the Lewd's home. Officer Strunk and Officer Waid. Strunk was a police veteran with twenty-nine years of service; Waid had been an officer just over a year.

* * *

Officer Strunk and Officer Waid bounded up the steps of Jason's house two days later at 9:45 a.m. They knocked at the front door. Jason opened the door and poked his head out. He did not look surprised to see two officers of the law on his doorstep.

"Yes, gentleman?"

"Sorry to bother you, sir," Officer Waid said. "Creekside reported one of their teachers hasn't shown for work the last two days. They—ah—they are concerned."

"I don't understand. Why are you here?"

"Apparently, the man knew your wife. Could we speak with her? We're simply trying to follow up every lead, you understand."

Jason frowned. "She isn't here," he said. "She went to visit her sister last Friday."

"Any reason she didn't tell the school her plans?"

"She doesn't work there anymore."

"I see." Officer Strunk looked at Jason as if sizing him up. "Why did she go see her sister?"

"She's ill. It came on suddenly."

"I see." The officer paused. "We'd like to look your place over, if you don't mind."

"No problem at all, officer. Come right in."

* * *

The officers performed a thorough search of the Lewd premises but found nothing unusual. There was no sign of either Marie or Rob, not that they had expected to find either of them. The house looked tidy. When asked if he had heard of Rob Sullivan, Jason looked puzzled. "Name sounds familiar," he said. "Marie might have mentioned him once."

Jason produced a picture of Marie's sister upon Officer Strunk's request. She was a thin woman, maybe thirty-five years old, with shoulder length red hair and green eyes.

"When will your wife be back?"

"Depends on how quickly Jill recovers." Not the slightest hesitation.

"What's wrong with her?"

"Exhaustion."

"Ok. We won't bother you any longer." They turned to go. But then Officer Waid turned back around and added: "Would you have your wife contact headquarters when she gets back? A few questions we'd like to ask."

"Certainly."

When they reached headquarters Officer Strunk wrote up his report. Five pages that said they'd found nothing. Probably Rob had run off with Lewd's wife, he thought. It happened all the time. One more year and he could retire. He was counting down the days.

* * *

The Sergeant read the report over carefully. "Seems all right."

Officer Strunk frowned. "Meaning?"

"We've run background checks on Lewd and his wife. The wife's as clean as a whistle. The husband is odd but harmless. His story checks out as well. Marie has an older sister named Jill. Don't know if she's sick or not but she was definitely the lady you describe in the photograph. She lives in Cleveland. If Mrs. Lewd returns we'll question her, but between you and me I doubt we'll see her or Sullivan again."

III

Peter Worth taught 5th grade at Creekside. He was the first person the police interviewed after Rob's disappearance. And they had reason to be interested in what he had to say. It was Peter who told them Rob was distressed when Marie left.

Peter had met Rob in graduate school at the University of Pittsburgh ten years before and the two became friends. Upon graduating, Rob took a position at Creekside. Peter received employment at a school in Illinois, but even then the two corresponded often. It was interesting to compare life at school during those early years and they were able to help each other when times were rough.

Peter married a girl of Irish heritage after a short engagement and Rob was best man.

"Your turn," Peter said to Rob weeks after the wedding. "Any prospects?"

"Perhaps," came an enigmatic reply.

When an opening became available at Creekside the following year, Peter applied and accepted immediately when an offer was made.

Peter and his wife lived about a mile from the Lewds in a small red brick house. Peter was aware of Rob's attraction to Marie and knew Rob had been upset by her resignation. Rob told Peter that Jason was a recluse and that he suspected relations between Marie and her husband were strained. Peter knew as well that Rob could be headstrong.

"This isn't like Rob," he told his wife one Sunday evening. "Call me crazy if you will, but I know Rob—he never simply up and disappears. Something is terribly wrong. And I'm going to find out what."

At nine o'clock the next morning Peter parked his car a block from the Lewd residence and waited. There were lights on in the house and the blinds had been pulled. At one point Peter observed someone peeking through the blinds, but he could not make out who it was. A few seconds later the person disappeared.

Two cars were in the driveway. Peter recognized Marie's red convertible. The police mentioned Marie might have left town to deal with an ill family member. So she had returned—but when? Peter didn't remember seeing the other car before, but assumed it was Jason's. Chances were both Marie and Jason were at home which was not good. Peter wanted to be sure Jason was not in the house. He wanted to talk to Marie alone.

Thick, dark thunderclouds rolled overhead. At one point, rain splattered against the windshield, but stopped after a few seconds. There was a pit in Peter's stomach and his right hand was trembling. He was about to give up and go home when the front door opened and Jason emerged. Peter trained a pair of binoculars on the object of his quest.

Peter had seen Jason once or twice before, when he went to the Lewd house to see Marie on school business. He had never liked the man. His face was scarred and weather-beaten, his hair disheveled, his hands enormous and covered with short, brown hairs. His eyes were light-blue and bloodshot and seemed to burn with rage. And he spoke in short, clipped phrases that were unnerving.

Jason looked nervously up and down the street while he fidgeted with his coat pocket. Then he got into his car and drove off.

Peter knew he did not have a moment to lose. He got out of the car and crossed the street, ran up the steps to the house. He rang the doorbell, but no one answered. He tried to open the door. It was locked. He went around to the back and tried the back door. Also locked. He looked inside through the dining room windows. He saw the dining room table with a vase of flowers on it. Off to one side was a piano and he recalled that Marie played occasionally at school events. He was turning to look for a side entrance when he heard a moan from inside the house.

He rapped on the window. "Hey!"

Another moan—no—it was more like a low wail. A long-drawn-out wail of unhappiness.

Something had been gnawing at Peter all morning and now he knew what it was. The day before Rob disappeared he had told Peter that Marie was unhappy. At the time Peter assumed Rob was referring to the period before Marie resigned. But now he wasn't so sure. It was just as likely Rob was referring to the present. And how would he have known she was unhappy if he was no longer in contact with her? He tried to force away the thoughts that flooded his mind but they only grew stronger.

Peter was not an impulsive man, but this time found himself acting without forethought. He picked up a rock and hurled it through the window. Then he picked up a stick and broke away the remaining shards of glass. He reached inside, unlocked the window, and pulled it open. Then he pulled himself up onto the sill and climbed through.

Silence.

"Anyone here?"

No response.

That's funny, Peter thought to himself. He was sure he had heard something. He figured that since he was inside the house he might as well have a look around.

He went into the kitchen and then the dining room. He examined the living room as well. There was a picture of Marie on the fireplace mantle. She was wearing a green sweater and was holding a bouquet of red roses. Her green eyes were bewitching. She looked so pretty—so happy, so content—that Peter could see why Rob was so fond of her.

A study off the living room contained an oak desk and a couch. He examined the papers on the desk. There was a bank statement and a telephone bill and a letter to—Jason's mother! Jason (he had signed the letter) had written that the weather in Pittsburgh was unbearable, that he was still looking for work, and that several possibilities had recently presented themselves. He didn't mention Marie.

Peter went back into the living room. On the living room sofa was a man's leather jacket. In one of the pockets Peter found a ticket to the horse races. It was dated the day before.

He glanced out the windows and saw an elderly couple walking arm-in-arm, an ice-cream truck, a boy on a bicycle. But no sign of Jason. The air in the room was deathly still. One could have heard a pin drop. Peter knew he should probably leave, but he couldn't bring himself to do so. There *had* to be something here.

He started up the stairs.

On the second floor there were two bedrooms and a bathroom. The bathroom was spotless. The tub sparkling, the towels freshly laundered. The first bedroom looked to be a guest room and Peter saw nothing unusual. It was in the second bedroom—the Lewd's bedroom—that he made a discovery. A piece of fabric underneath the bed. A piece he recognized as coming from the shirt Rob had been wearing the day before he disappeared. He remembered the material for it was made from Egyptian cotton (Rob had mentioned it proudly). Peter had never felt anything so soft and he recalled commenting on it at the time.

He searched the room looking for something—anything—that would tell him what had happened to his friend. He looked behind furniture and underneath the bed. He searched through the dressers and a chest of drawers. He opened the large walk-in closet and went inside. Nothing.

Just then he smelled something funny—a stale smell in the air. He glanced up at the ceiling and saw a hatch. An opening to the attic, no doubt. The hatch was made of plywood that had been painted a bright green, a brighter color than the dull green the rest of the closet had been painted. And it looked fresh. But that wasn't all Peter observed. There was something else. The hatch was ajar—it hadn't been closed properly—and through the crack he saw drops of blood. Drops of blood that were slowly forming.

Peter felt nauseated, but he knew what he had to do. He went out into the hall and got an old wicker chair he had seen there and he brought it back into the closet. He got up on the chair and opened the hatch. Then he pulled himself up into the attic.

And he screamed.

Facing him, like a hideous gorgon, was the decomposing body of Rob Sullivan. The poor man's throat had been slashed and blooded still dripped from the wound.

Interlude

"It seems an odd place to hide a body," I interjected.

"It's happens more than one might think," Charles replied with a smile. "How many times have the bones of a wife been found in the attic after the death of the husband? And vice-versa. Why, there was a case in Florida once where—"

"Enough!" I cried. "I get your point."

"Besides," he continued, "in all likelihood Jason expected a visit from the police. Marie had left Creekside and Rob was missing. Jason suspected an affair and he must have felt the police would uncover evidence of one as well. And that would lead them straight to him for questioning. He couldn't very well bury the body in his backyard so he hid it in the place he thought least likely to be searched. And it turns out he was right. At least as far as the police were concerned."

Charles picked up his coffee mug and took a sip. Then he continued with his story.

IV

A single thought raced through Peter's mind: *Get out!* In a flash, he rushed down the steps to the first floor. He was white as a ghost and shaking uncontrollably. The police would have to be notified at once. And he did not dare stay in the house a moment longer. Jason might return at any moment—the madman who had murdered his best friend and done who knows what with Marie. He shuddered.

He opened the front door, had one foot out the door, when he heard it again: a low, quivering wail, like that of a ghost.

And it was coming from the basement.

Oh, my God, Peter thought. Something's down there. He was as terrified as ever but there was no question of leaving now. The steps that led to the basement were located off the kitchen. He turned on the light and started down.

The steps creaked ominously. There was a wooden railing he held tightly as he descended. He had been afraid of basements ever since he was a child. The darkness and the musty air. Rodents who lurked in the shadows.

But he had to put those fears behind him. There was a child's rocking horse at the foot of the stairs (this

Peter found odd for he knew that the Lewds had no children). A bookcase against the wall behind it. Even though the light was on it seemed quite dim. The air was musty. There was an oil furnace which cast grotesque shadows on the wall. A deer's head mounted on the wall facing him. Beside it a gun cabinet. He did not like the looks of things at all.

He saw a door that led to another room. And before he realized what was happening the doorknob was in his hand and he opened the door.

He had come upon Marie. She was bound and gagged and her eyes were filled with terror.

He pulled out a pocketknife and cut away her bonds. She threw her arms around him and began sobbing. Her face was pale. There were cuts on her arms and neck and her clothes were filthy.

"Let's get out of here," Peter said. "There's no time to lose." He took her hands and pulled her back through the door.

It was dark. That was odd. He could have sworn he hadn't touched the light switch. Just then he thought he heard something moving in the darkness. Something large and ominous. His heart beat uncontrollably. He felt his hands beginning to sweat.

He held Marie's hands tightly and pulled her closer to him. Just then the lights came on and Peter found himself staring into the lunatic eyes of Jason Lewd. The crazy man threw his head back and laughed.

"My husband," Marie sobbed.

Jason's laughter slowly dissolved into a fit of maniacal fury. His eyes darted back and forth between Peter and Marie. "Ha! Ha!" he cried. "Another one!" A gun flashed in his hands and he began waving it around. Marie was hysterical. Peter did not know what to do. He was confronted by a madman and there appeared to be no way out. And so—

He lunged towards Jason and the gun went off.

"No!" It was Marie. "For God's sake, Jason, stop!"

Peter lay wounded at Jason's feet. He looked up into the eyes of a man who was no longer human.

"Don't—"

Jason emptied the gun into the dying man. Then his hand fell to his side and he dropped the gun on the floor. It clattered and was still. He stared at the dead man, watched in fascination as blood flowed from the wounds and pooled on the floor. There were beads of sweat on Jason's forehead and his eyes were glassy and his face was pale.

He turned to face Marie. The color had drained from her face. Every muscle in his body was tense.

She backed up against the gun cabinet. "Jason," she said. "Jason, please. My God, Jason." His hands were upraised; he would strangle her, she knew. "Jason! Jason!"

She turned the handle of the cabinet and—thank God—it opened, making a creaking sound as it did so. Luckily, he did not notice.

Marie knew her husband kept his weapons loaded. He always had to be ready, he told her once, but for what she never knew. She called out to him again as she groped for a weapon and finding one held it tightly, her fingers on cold steel.

She hissed: "Jason, Jason." Three shots at point-blank range into the body of her husband who uttered a cry and collapsed onto the floor. He was writhing in pain and his face registered astonishment. "Jason! Jason!" Two more shots and he moved no more.

* * *

Thirty minutes later the police found her there, curled up on the floor in the fetal position. They had been alerted to the disturbance by a neighbor who heard shots.

Two dead men and a woman who would not speak for days. The truth came out in the end, as it usually does in these sorts of cases. It turns out that Jason had been unable to allay his suspicions and had confronted

Marie over her alleged infidelities. She denied everything, but he did not believe her. He forced her to leave Creekside—Marie said he threatened to kill her if she did not do so.

Jason began drinking and at times became violent. Without Marie's income money was tight. He tried to alleviate their financial woes by embezzling small amounts of cash from work. When he lost his job, he started gambling. Marie found out about it one day and when she confronted her husband he locked her away.

There was an investigation, but it was determined that Marie acted in self-defense and she was not charged. She moved to California and eventually remarried.

Epilogue

"That's a pretty sad story, it's true," I said. "However, I don't see how it proves your point."

"Let me put it to you bluntly: would you say Marie was justified in shooting her husband?"

I bolted from my chair. "Of course she was justified! He was going to murder her just as he had—"

"Her lover?"

"There was nothing between them, you said so quite clearly."

"Yes, but Jason thought there was."

"And that justifies his actions?"

"Perhaps not. But it does explain them."

"Surely you aren't saying that Jason was justified in murdering two innocent people. If so—why, then, you are as mad as he!"

"But don't you see?" Charles said and his eyes glowed like orbs of fire. "Jason was led to imprison his wife by his belief that she was having an affair. Rob was led to search for Marie by his concern for her. Peter was led to investigate Rob's disappearance by his devotion to his friend. And Marie was led by the cumulative weight of all of that to pull the trigger on the gun that sealed her fate. We may call Jason's deed evil, or Marie's for that matter, but it was no more evil than the drawing of your next breath. It was preordained. Fixed. Immutable."

"Preposterous. There is quite a difference between Jason's actions and Marie's. On the one hand you're talking about a normal human reaction—self-defense—on the other you're talking about cold-blooded murder."

"It's only a matter of degree."

I frowned. "*That* I can never accept."

"Let us agree then to disagree."

I nodded.

"Oh, there one was other thing," Charles said. "During the investigation, Marie was asked why she resigned her position at Creekside instead of simply informing the police she was being hounded by her husband. She was a strong woman and by all accounts loved her job. Was it possible something else was going on, some activity of a criminal nature—gambling perhaps?—that they were *both* involved in and that had gone sour."

"That's preposterous!" I cried. "The woman was scared. But let's assume—for the sake of argument—that something else *was* going on. Even so, it's quite clear Marie acted in self-defense."

"You mean she said that she did."

I paused. "Hmm," I said. "I see your point."

"My only point is that life's a muddle," Charles concluded.

We said our good-byes then and he went outside into the cold October night.

I brewed myself a cup of lapsang tea and sat before the roaring fire, thinking about what Charles had said. I was troubled, to be sure. I knew the man did not speak lightly, that he meant every word he said. Even so, I could not accept his argument. To do so meant a world in disarray. Chaos. And what arises out of chaos but anarchy?

"Everything is relative," Charles had intoned. "As the great Einstein once said. Many events happen by chance. The man who is a saint could just as easily be a sinner—and may in fact be one when looked at in this light instead of that one. Look!"—he fairly shouted the word—"Look at your own hand. Tomorrow will it deliver a loving caress or will it choke the life from—"

I imagine a world with no rules, with no laws, where everything is simultaneously permissible and forbidden. A world where nothing is black and white, where everything is gray. Perhaps Charles was right. Perhaps that was the world in which I found myself.

"It's a matter of principle," I had insisted. "There *are* eternal truths."

But now, as I stare into the flames of a fire that rise higher and higher, I wonder: what if I am wrong? And then I realize that if I am wrong—and Charles is right—I may as well be right and Charles wrong, that is, that the question has no meaning. Oh, bother. Charles was right about one thing: this is a town without pity.

SKIPPING STONES

The rains of the previous week had ceased. For seven days and seven nights—a relentless fury. It was mid-afternoon. Big, black birds slowly circled in a tarantula sky. The slow-moving creek that ran by their house had swelled to twice its normal size and Laura watched in morbid fascination as frenzied waters rushed by. She picked up a stone—a flat white stone, the kind good for skipping—and slung it into the water, but the current was swift and it refused to hop.

"Laura."

She turned, saw her father at the top of the hill. He was dressed in his favorite white suit with the tan fedora. His eyes somber. A scowl upon his face.

"Yes, Father?"

"Are you coming?"

"In a minute."

She turned back to face the water. She had no desire to return to the house. She knew what her father wanted and she could not acquiesce. Not now. There was a stick lying several feet from her and she picked it up and tossed it into the brackish water. It swung about, buffeted by the current, then disappeared around a bend in the creek. She climbed up onto the granite rock that overlooked the creek like a vulture. It was the place she came to when she needed to get away. The rock was shaped like an hourglass with a hollowed-out section in the middle in which she would sit and look out over the creek. Like a captain surveying the open sea. When she had first come upon the rock she thought that perhaps it had been sculpted by an artist from long ago. It certainly seemed out-of-place on a bank covered with thousands of skipping stones. She had asked her mother about it once, but the woman merely shrugged and told her not to worry about such things.

She remembered her mother, her long, wavy hair, her amber eyes. That gentle way she had of speaking. She had never known a more gracious person, nor one filled with such self-confidence. Her mother had an advanced degree in chemistry, but never sought employment in the field. She married John while in college. Laura was born a year later. She would stay home with the child, she said. Her career could wait. The child could not. She had sacrificed everything for her family. And yet had Laura ever really appreciated that with which she had been graced?

She lay on her back and looked up into the discolored sky, so narrow and dense. She closed her eyes and her thoughts melted away.

When she awoke, the sun was low in the sky. She frowned. It must have been nearly five o'clock and they would all be gone. Her father would be furious, of course. She hopped down off the rock and brushed off her clothes. Then she picked up another stone and tossed it into the creek. Ker-plunk it went as it fell into the water with a splash, concentric rings flowing out from the point of impact. Another followed and then another and then another. Ker-plunk, ker-plunk, ker-plunk.

She trudged up the winding path that led to the house. The path was muddy from the recent rains and by the time she reached the house her shoes were caked with red mud. She took them off and went inside, walked trembling down the long hallway that led to her father's study. The study door was open and she went inside, saw the green armchair and the majestic oak desk that her father said she would inherit when he died.

She would apologize for not coming to the house when Catherine was there. She had been sleeping (or dreaming) down by the creek and had lost track of time. It would not happen again. But when the green chair pivoted and she saw the stern face of her father, she shut up like a clam. He picked up a cigar and puffed at it. He wanted her to begin but she was silent. A fly buzzed near him and he swatted it away.

He asked why she had not come before and she tried to apologize. But he interrupted, told her she had been rude. He was right, she said, and as she looked at the wooden floor she felt his angry eyes upon her. He wanted to know why she would not accept Catherine—didn't she realize she was hurting him? His voice was filled with reproach. It was all too much for Laura. Her cheeks were bathed in tears.

He told her to leave; he did not want to look at her. She left the study and went to her bedroom. She fell upon the bed and cried, icy tears sliding down her cheeks. Her body trembled as waves of emotion surged. It was as if a knife had cut her open from within. She forced herself to rise and was startled to find the room slanting awkwardly. It was deathly silent. She breathed deeply. One. Two. Three. Then she dried her eyes and went to the closet and picked out her favorite dress, the bright yellow one with ruffled sleeves, and a dark-blue sweater with white buttons down the front and she returned to the creek where she could be alone. Her right hand was trembling and she tried to control it, but it would not be still.

Dusk was approaching and a yellow fog was settling over the creek. The speed of the current had not abated. If anything the water flowed faster now and the water level was higher. She reached down and touched the water. It was icy cold. She shivered and pulled back her hand. She picked up a flat rock, white and smooth. She flicked it into the water, throwing it with the current. It hit the water at just the right angle and skipped twice before disappearing into the depths.

She thought about the last time she had seen her mother. At the funeral. Her mother was wearing a red dress. A pearl necklace Laura had given her on her thirty-eighth birthday. She never looked more beautiful, Laura thought. Lying in her coffin. Uncle Bob came over and put his arm around her. He told her about the time her mother brought her home from the hospital. A pretty girl with serious blue eyes and a warm smile. That is how he described her. He had never seen his sister look so happy, he said. Nor John so proud. Everyone, it seemed, was crying. One of the happiest days of their lives.

Laura smiled.

Yes, Laura, he said to her softly, you must never forget. Promise me you will never forget.

Uncle Bob moved away on the arms of Aunt Ruth and two of her cousins came over. Jenny with her freshly scrubbed cheeks and her iridescent eyes. Steve with his fine, dark hair and his elegant hands. Steve who three years later was to die—like her mother—in a freak car accident. Oh, Lord. Why did her mother have to go out that night? Why did she take that route to the grocery store? Why did she swerve to avoid whatever it was she felt she had to avoid? Why did she do exactly what she did? Only questions, of course. There were always only questions.

Her fondest memories. She remembered how her mother used to bake bread on Sunday afternoons. She would climb atop the counter and watch as her mother kneaded the dough and rolled it out into loaves and put the loaves into pans. While the bread rose, they would tell riddles and play word games and Laura would reveal her dreams and then she asked her mother about her own childhood. She was always asking questions, her mother said. Lord, she had never heard so many questions. Now she saw her mother before her. Her bright face. Her pretty figure. Her smile that had always filled her with warmth. She was so smart, so elegant. Nothing stopped her, she thought. Nothing.

Her mother was speaking:

"I'll never forget the day, Laura, when I was walking across the tobacco fields, minding my own business. It was the month of July, the air hot and sticky. I saw the cows and the chickens, happy pigs rolling in red mud, and I saw that wretched farmer. He was the meanest man I'd ever met, his eyes dark and filled with rage. He saw me and hollered. I was wearing my red dress with the ruffles on the sleeves. A yellow sunbonnet. That man never liked me. He thought I was out to steal his hens. And so I did. Just to spite him. He found out it was me and he talked to my parents and I had to apologize and I wasn't let out of the house for a week. And you won't believe it, Laura, but I talked to the farmer's wife later on. She was a charming woman, intelligent, worldly—not what I'd imagined her to be. She told me her husband had always admired me. A spunky girl, he called me. And her husband was a good man. With a kind heart and as honest as anyone she'd known. If he appeared bitter (she seemed to be able to read my mind) it was only because he saw in me what he would never have. She didn't elaborate, but I knew what she meant. And it was then I realized that people are often not what you take them to be. Are often quite different." She smiled and looked off into the distance. Remembering.

Laura recalled the time her father introduced her to Catherine. It had been over a year ago, yet it seemed as if it was yesterday. Hello, Laura, pleased to meet you. John has told me much about you. Why, just now he was saying how proud he is . . . And her voice trailed off into oblivion for Laura would not listen to another word. How many times had they gone out together before she moved in with them? Half-a-dozen, perhaps. No more. And what had been Laura's impression? Catherine was a kind woman, certainly. A sympathetic woman. A gentle usurper. Laura had wanted to talk to her father about her feelings but she never found the courage. And he . . . what had he wanted? He never confided in her. She did not know what he felt—could only imagine. He missed his wife, certainly, he had never been the same since she died . . . but . . . but what? That he wanted Laura to forget? That he wanted her to be happy? Didn't he know that she would never forget, that she would never be happy? That she was drowning in unhappiness?

She looked into the mauve twilight so steady and peaceful. A cool wind was blowing and the pine trees looked like matchsticks as they gently swayed. Her concentration was broken by the cries of a flock of birds overhead. She looked up into the opalescent light of dusk and saw them there and she could not help herself but she began to cry once again. She felt as if she was floating in a sea of dark jelly. Surrounded by waters of loneliness, there were no stars to guide her.

Laura. Laura.
Yes, Father?
Are you coming?
No, Father, I will never come.

She had nothing against Catherine, really. (Catherine with her long brown hair and her hazel eyes and her perfect manners.) And she wanted her father to be happy. (Her father. What was there she could say to him? Without hurting herself. Without hurting them all.) But . . . But what? Was it simply that Catherine was not her mother? That she was not her? That is what they all thought, of course. But that was not it, would never be it. Yet how could she put it into words? That which could not be explained, could only be felt. It was the way things stood. That no matter how much she might have wished otherwise, there was nothing she could do or say that would satisfy them. And it would never change.

The art of stone skipping had no beginning and no end. Dapping, skiffing, ricochet. Ducks and drakes. Every language had its own word, but the physics was the same the world over. What did it mean to skip stones? You took a stone, a flat stone, about the size of your palm, smooth of course and oval, and you slung it into the water. If released at precisely the right angle, fast and with plenty of downward force, it ricocheted off the water, sweeping out a long parabolic arc. Several times, if you possessed enough skill. Or if you were lucky. Defying gravity. She'd done a four-skip once. Of that she'd been quite proud. But usually it was only two or three. She wasn't very good at skipping stones.

She loved this time of day when everything was changing. She closed her eyes and saw not the blackness of the night which was fast approaching but the whiteness of infinity. Like a winter snowstorm. She saw the ghost of her mother in the distance and she called to her but her voice was drowned out by the sound of Catherine laughing. A cold, cruel laugh sharp as hail. She clung to the granite rock as if it were a lifeline. Everything, it seemed, was dissolving.

She thought about what there would be if she could choose what there would be. There would be no girlfriend, no Catherine, no love affair. There would be nothing, nothing.

"If you were to ask me, Father, I'd say she's very much in love with you," Laura said, her voice a mere whisper. "You're both very much in love."

She slipped into the raging water, like a swan.

MARIO BAKAR

In a distant land, on a faraway shore, there lived a young merchant named Mario Bakar. He spent his days traveling from town to town, selling handmade rugs in bazaars, and though he was not known for the quality of his work, his prices were low and he somehow managed to eke out a living.

Bakar lived in the town of Safi, which is located on the west coast of Morocco. He was unmarried, but had his eyes set on a beautiful young woman named Maria who, unfortunately, had her eyes set on a handsome man named Roberto. In fact, the two were engaged! Their upcoming marriage was the talk of the town and wedding festivities had already begun.

At the moment my story begins Bakar was walking alone on the beach, gazing out at the great, blue sea—and wondering if he should end his life right then and there. What a glorious death, he thought, to drown at sea out of love for a woman! But Bakar was a coward and could not bring himself to make that fateful plunge. He decided to go fishing instead; it was the best way he knew to calm his nerves: to spend several hours gazing out at the sea, that greatest expanse of all, to see what treasures he could extract from it. Bakar had brought a pole and bait and now he sat on a large rock at the water's edge and cast his line. Not a minute had gone by when he felt a tug at the end of the pole. Excitedly, he reeled in his catch. He was not disappointed. It was a beautiful fish: light pink in color, with a long head, slender body, and a delicately curved fin. It must have been at least four feet long. Bakar had never seen such a remarkable fish and he stared in awe as it flapped back and forth at the end of the line, imagining himself as a great fisherman.

When his reveries ended, Bakar laid the fish on the beach and pulled out his knife. He placed the blade on the fish's throat—intending to put it out of its misery—when, to his amazement, the fish spoke:

"Mario," it said. "Spare my life and I shall make you rich beyond your wildest dreams."

Bakar realized this was not an ordinary fish, but a god disguised as a fish, and obligingly, he pulled away the knife.

"Put me back in the sea," said the fish, "and out of gratitude I will grant you three wishes; whatever you desire shall be yours."

Bakar unhooked the fish from the end of the line and threw it back in the water. The fish leaped from wave to wave, so happy was it to have regained its freedom, and then it disappeared into the sea, never to be seen by Bakar again.

Bakar's first impulse was to wish for ten million dirhams so as never to worry for lack of money and then for a harem of beautiful wives so as never to worry for lack of affection and then for the rebirth of his father who had died when Bakar was twelve and whom he had loved so dearly. But it occurred to him that then he would have used up all his wishes—the very wishes he had been granted only moments before. Being a prudent man, Bakar deemed it best to see what the future held in store for him before spending any of his precious gifts.

* * *

Several months passed. Maria and Roberto were now married. It had been one of the most magnificent marriages Safi had ever witnessed, filled with merry feasts and celebration; even now, weeks after the blessed event, the papers were filled with news concerning the newly-weds: that Roberto had taken a vow never to leave Maria's sight; that the joyous cries of their lovemaking could be heard from miles around; that Maria was already with child. Bakar tried not to pay attention to any of this (none of it was true, though Bakar did not know this), but it was nearly impossible and he found himself thinking more and more about what their life together would have been like.

Bakar still had to work for a living and one day he found himself at a bazaar in the town of Marrakech, selling his wares as usual. Imagine his amazement when Roberto and Maria approached his table and began looking over his selection of handmade rugs. They were furnishing their new home, they said, and had in mind a large order. Preoccupied with shopping, the newlyweds did not seem to recognize Bakar, who himself was not about to say a word. They looked so happy together—Maria on Roberto's arm—Bakar could only grit his teeth and look away.

Suddenly, Roberto spoke up in dismay, "These rugs are worthless. They look like they were stitched by a five-year-old."

Bakar stiffened. He did not know what upset him more: that Roberto did not appreciate the months of toil which had gone into his weaving, that his already languishing business was about to languish further, or that he had been publicly insulted—and in front of Maria, no less, whom he loved dearly. He shrugged but said nothing. What could he say that would not but make matters worse?

Roberto turned to Maria and said, "Let's go. We're only wasting our time at this table."

They had turned to leave when Bakar, who was about to burst into tears, blurted out, "No, sir! My rugs are of the finest quality. You'll find none better—I swear." And he muttered under his breath, "Or so I wish it."

"He's speaking the truth," said an old man busy examining Bakar's goods. "These are without a doubt the most beautiful rugs I've ever seen!"

The townspeople, who had gathered around Bakar's table when the argument broke out, echoed their agreement:

"These rugs have such wonderful patterns," one woman said.

"And such bright colors—so bold and clear," said a young girl.

Bakar looked down at the rugs and saw that it was true: any flaws had been magically corrected: the rugs were perfect works of art!

Bakar was all smiles. "And the prices are low!" he exclaimed.

"I'll take this one," said a voice.

"And I this one," said someone else.

Bakar was beside himself with joy. Indeed, he had nearly forgotten about Maria and Roberto, so preoccupied was he serving customers; but then he saw the two of them out of the corner of his eye, arguing fiercely.

"You fool!" cried Maria. "They're wonderful rugs—and at a good price—but in a moment they'll be gone and we'll have none. And all because you're jealous of Bakar!"

So she did recognize me! thought Bakar and his heart leaped into his mouth.

Maria's words touched off howls of protest from Roberto and he began pelting her with blows. Bakar tried to go to her aid, but he was surrounded by people showering money upon him and he could not get near. Luckily, two policemen arrived on the scene and they carted Roberto away.

The crowd parted. Maria rushed into Bakar's arms and showered him with kisses—you see, she had secretly loved Bakar all along, but had been forced by her father to marry Roberto to pay back a debt owed the young man's family.

But that meant nothing now, for the would-be lovers had been united at last.

Bakar and Maria were married shortly thereafter. And so the first wish was fulfilled.

* * *

Oh, glorious wedding day! That most holy of days when a man and woman are united in the blessed bonds of matrimony, when they proclaim to the world that they shall be husband and wife, each to the other lover and loved, till death do they part.

Unfortunately, for our bride and groom—for Maria and Bakar—all was not well. What by all accounts should have been a glorious honeymoon had turned into a disaster. There they sat, perched on the edge of the marital bed like two sour-faced peasants: Bakar trembling, Maria frowning. For, you see, the size of Bakar's sex was several sizes too small! Maria had been spoiled by the sexual conquistador that was Roberto, a magnificent lover whose romantic exploits were well-chronicled in the epic works of poets and balladeers. She tried to hide her disappointment—after all, this was the man she loved—but it was too late, Bakar had sensed her displeasure. And so he said to himself (and this time he knew what he was doing): "I wish I were twice as big." No sooner had he done so than his sexual organ began to grow—not one, not two, but three sizes larger! Maria uttered a cry of delight as she watched her lover's love grow more lovely. Bakar uttered a sigh of relief realizing the evening had been saved. He smiled broadly and prepared to mount his beautiful mare. Moments later the two settled down into what proved to be a sleepless night of passionate lovemaking, a magical night they would remember forever.

And so the second wish was fulfilled.

* * *

From that night forward the Bakar family prospered and multiplied—five children in ten years was the end result. Bakar's rug business flourished as well and soon he was forced to hire a dozen helpers. After forty years Bakar sold the business for ten million dirhams to a group of entrepreneurs headquartered in the nearby town of El Jadida. Wishing to help the community in which he had lived so long, he decided to run for mayor of Safi. He won, in a landslide victory, and served three consecutive terms. The town prospered under Bakar's leadership and when he left office a parade was held in his honor: Mr. and Mrs. Bakar riding a beautiful white float that was decorated with the petals of a thousand roses!

The Bakars retired to a home on the outskirts of Safi, perched atop a hill overlooking the ocean. One would have thought their remaining years would have been peaceful and harmonious, free of all worries and cares, but Bakar's life very nearly came to a tragic end.

One evening he was walking on the beach, enjoying the solitude of the sea and the heavenly stars above, when without warning he was attacked by a band of hooligans wielding sticks and knives. They demanded all of Bakar's money and, when they discovered he had none, knocked him to the ground and beat him mercilessly. Bakar pleaded for his life, but they only laughed. "Stupid old man!" one of them said.

It was then Bakar remembered the wishes: his life with Maria had been so prosperous he had forgotten all about them. But had he any left? And if he did, was his protector still listening? He took a deep breath, then cried out with all his might, "I wish you were all dead!"

At once there was a crack of thunder, louder than any that had been heard in Safi before and, from out of the star filled sky, came six lightning bolts, one for each hooligan, turning them into six piles of smoldering ashes.

And so the third wish was fulfilled.

* * *

It was nearly a decade later when Bakar (who was nearly eighty years old) lay on his deathbed, attended to by Maria, who was weeping tears of grief. Bakar had caught a chill one evening when walking alone on the beach two miles from his home. An unexpected squall had arisen from the north, pelting him with wind and rain. It took Bakar nearly an hour before he reached home and by then he was shivering uncontrollably. His condition seemed to stabilize that night, but the next day took a turn for the worse. It was pneumonia, the doctors said. There was nothing they could do.

People came from miles around to say farewell to this man they so greatly respected. Outwardly calm (they did not want to upset Bakar while he was preparing for death), but inwardly filled with grief, they could only wish him well on his upcoming journey. At one point such a throng had assembled outside the Bakar home that Bakar was carried on his deathbed out to the village square so all could bear witness to his final moments. It was on the third day of this gathering of souls that a young boy, not realizing the solemnity of the occasion, asked Bakar the secret of his long and happy life.

Up until this point Bakar had said not a word, but now he raised himself from the bed as if he intended to speak. A hush fell over the crowd. Would the child be reprimanded? Bakar turned to the boy and smiled.

"One must always live by the sea," he said, his voice raspy, his eyelids drooping. Then he fell back upon the bed with a groan and breathed no more.

The wails of the crowd which went out at that moment were not noticed by the boy who, upon hearing Bakar's words, had started down to the sea in search of his own treasure.

TWO BRIEF LOVE STORIES

1. A Love Story

Phil goes to a bar where he meets Sally. They hit it off and after talking for several hours they return to Phil's apartment where they have sex which they both find satisfying. They repeat this procedure once a week for the next two months. At this point Sally agrees to move in with Phil. The move goes smoothly; several of Sally and Phil's friends even help out. Things seem to be going well.

On their first anniversary, they go to a restaurant for dinner. They dress up; Sally has never looked more beautiful, nor Phil more handsome. Sally suspects that Phil is about to propose.

The food is delicious, the service superb. Their waiter delights them with a juggling act done with forks and knives. Sally laughs and rubs her foot against Phil's. Phil looks at Sally. Sally looks at Phil. This is it.

Sally says to Phil, "I love you." Phil says to Sally, "Yes." What does this mean? That, yes, Phil loves Sally? Or that, yes, Phil knows that Sally loves Phil? Or that Phil has simply recognized the predicate Sally has uttered? Or is this simply an equivocation on Phil's part? Is it all or part or none of these things? You can see that the possibilities are endless. And what is Sally to make of this, what is Sally to think? Regardless of what Sally thinks Phil has said, or rather, meant, Sally's reply to Phil's equivocation is certain to be equally equivocal. And so on, ad infinitum, until neither is saying a word the other understands, though each thinks the other understands perfectly. At this point Sally and Phil both sigh dreamily, each thinking that what they wished to hear was what in fact they heard.

The troubles begin. Phil feels trapped. Phil considers embarking upon another relationship, with Joan, but decides against it. Phil cares deeply about Sally; in fact, there is no one Phil cares more about right now than Sally, though Phil is not prepared to make a lifelong commitment to Sally at this time. Even so, Phil is not himself. Sally suspects an affair and confronts Phil. Phil denies any involvement. Phil says it is Sally not he who has changed. Sally threatens to move out. Phil tells Sally to go ahead. Sally starts to cry. Phil shouts this is all Sally's fault. Now, both are crying.

Phil says to Sally, "You no longer love me." Sally says to Phil, "Yes." What does this mean? That, yes, Sally no longer loves Phil? Or that, yes, Sally knows that Phil thinks that Sally no longer loves Phil? Or that Sally has simply recognized the predicate Phil has uttered? Or is this simply an equivocation on Sally's part? Is it all or part or none of these things? You can see that the possibilities are endless. And what is Phil to make of all this, what is Phil to think? At this point Phil is so frustrated over the current state of their relationship that he shouts back in anger, "No, you never loved me!" Sally reciprocates with equal ferocity. The conversation deteriorates from there until both throw up their hands in disgust and agree to go their separate ways.

2. Worms

How was work today?" Pam asks as she sits down at the dining room table. Her husband doesn't answer. He rarely does these days. Not right away. It takes several minutes for him to decompress. Roger Stockton works at the dockyards, loading freight. It's a job he's held nearly twenty years. It is hard work, and though it has never allowed them to accumulate savings, at least it pays the bills.

Now he sits in his chair at the head of the dining room table and chews his meat. Slowly. Savoring every bite.

He chews loudly, Pam thinks.

She's made lamb stew with broccoli and corn muffins and a tossed Caesar salad. His favorite meal.

Still, he is silent. He doesn't like to talk when he's eating.

"I went shopping with Rachel today," Pam says.

"Um."

"We went to Woolworths and guess who we saw at the cosmetics counter?—why, Henrietta was there and you know what she told us—"

"Um."

"—she said she was leaving Harold! She called him an old goat."

"You don't say."

Dear me, she thinks. He isn't listening to a word.

"How was work?" she repeats.

He pauses, put down his fork down on the plate and picks up his napkin and wipes his mouth.

"You don't say!" he repeats and then he cackles. That cackle she had fallen in love with years before and which now she can't stand.

"Food okay?"

"Um."

"It's your favorite."

He pauses, scratches his chin. "I guess it depends," he says.

"Depends on what?"

"Depends on my mood."

At times like these—she's learned from experience—it is best to change the subject. "Rachel recommended this butcher shop. Maude's. She insists they're the best in town. Not cheap, though, that's for sure."

"You know what people say?"

It is one of his favorite games. She never knows what is to follow. But she has to play along.

"No," she says. "What do people say?"

"There's not a meal some people don't like." He bites into a muffin, chews. "They say some people even like to eat worms."

He guffaws once again.

"Turns out Harold was *cheating* on Henrietta," she says, ignoring him. She found a picture of the girl in his wallet. A young thing. Not even that attractive. And you know—"

Her husband snaps to attention. "What was she doing in his wallet?"

This time it is Pam who doesn't seem to hear. "— and you know what Rachel said?"

Roger is eating again. He looks at her with steely eyes.

"She said Henrietta was better off without him. And she's right. Henrietta's a smart girl. Works at the library. Just got a raise. She can support herself. Luckily they don't have children."

"Ours are gone."

He speaks the words sharply. Pointedly. As if they are an indictment.

"What do you mean by that?" Pam says, startled.

His fork rattles uncontrollably. "Nothing," he says. "I didn't mean nothing by it. Just that our kids are gone." He wipes his mouth, rises from the table, and goes into the living room. Moments later the television is blaring.

Pam goes into the study and reads until her eyelids are drooping. Then she takes a shower and crawls exhausted into bed. It is just past eleven. She turns out the light. As she pulls the blue cotton sheets over her head, she realizes that the television is still on and her husband has probably fallen asleep on the couch. This isn't the first time that has happened.

It would be nice to know what he did today, she thinks, as sleep slowly descends upon her. It really would be nice to know.

THE HOUSE IN THE FOREST

They said the house in the forest was haunted. They said an old woman and her husband lived there many years before, that they bickered endlessly, that she murdered him one gusty autumn night—poisoned him with blueberry muffins laced with cyanide—but was not found guilty beyond a reasonable doubt and now lived alone in a one-story house in the back woods of South Carolina where the days were cloaked in shadows and the nights were filled with shifting sounds. A prisoner in the soughing forest.

They said.

My sister Jill and I loved to roam through the forest after school. Valhalla was a primeval forest filled with maple and oak and pine. The scent of honeysuckle, spicebush, and partridgeberry floated on the air. We pretended we were detectives as we tracked unsavory characters along the trails and underbrush. There was Mr. Big, the notorious criminal from Texas, a man who was always on the run. Aunt Mary, Cousin Jeff, and Uncle John: the outlaw gang from Mississippi. Their latest heist: a bank robbery in the north of the state. Perhaps they had come to South Carolina to stash the loot? And then there was T-Bone Frank. Six feet ten with meaty hands, lumberjack arms, and nerves of steel. He had blood in his eyes and was rumored to have killed a man in Charleston. Who knew what he was up to now? We never caught anyone, of course, for they existed only in our imagination, but even so we had endless days of fun.

There was a river that ran through the forest, the water of which was the color of burnt copper. Jill and I would go there and stand upon the clay that formed the river's bank, observe the weeds swaying beneath the gentle current, the white polished stones that looked like dinosaur eggs, the silver fish that hid amongst them, search for pirate treasure that was rumored to be buried nearby. Treasure that we never found. But it was in the lurking shadows of a dreary rock that lay near the river that we found the note addressed to us, the children of the forest. *Be careful*, was all it said.

We were always careful to avoid the house in the forest for it was rumored that the old woman kidnapped children and we both knew what she did with them. We played many games together in the dappled light under the pine trees. Hide-and-Go-Seek, Hopscotch, Sticks-and-Stones. We talked of many things. Of what we would become when we grew up. Of the adventures we would undertake. Of what the world would look like. Soon my thoughts were lost in the swirl of dreams, but always the old woman loomed in the back of my mind.

One day my sister dared me to go into the forest at night. It was late in the month of October. The sky was dotted with clouds. The air cool and crisp. Leaves had fallen all around, forming a soft carpet on the forest floor. Might we catch a glimpse of the old woman knitting by the fireplace? When night fell, we entered the forest about one hundred yards from the house, crawled on our hands and knees, the twigs cracking like pistol shots. I was scared stiff, but I managed to conceal my fear. It was my sister who reached the house first and when she did so the moon emerged from behind a cloud. It was a gibbous moon the color of lead.

The house in the forest was made of stone. The windows were small, many-paned and high-up from the ground. One end of the house had a large stained-glass window that emitted a tenuous glow in the pale light of the moon. Smoke billowed from the chimney. A gravel walkway overgrown with weeds led up to a dimly lit front door. There was a light on inside the house and I could imagine the old lady seated in her rocking chair, a loaded shotgun across her lap. I watched as Jill made her way through the wild hawthorn bushes that surrounded the house, climbed atop an iron railing, and peered through a half-opened window.

She could see into the living room and she called back to me that it was empty. She observed that the walls were painted a dull yellow and cobwebs were visible above a doorway. A large painting hung on one wall. It looked like a painting of an elderly couple, she said. A count and countess perhaps. The woman was portrayed in vibrant red colors that seemed to snake into her soul, while the man blazed black as midnight, lending to each one the aspects of fire and of death. My sister glanced back at me and laughed. "Sissy," she said. "Your eyes look as though they're about to pop out of their sockets."

"Well," I said. "Where is she?" I felt a knot in my stomach.

She paused. "Want to go inside?"

I felt the earth quivering like jelly beneath my feet. "Go ahead."

She was through the window in a flash and I, reluctantly, followed.

It was in the bedroom that we found her. A little woman with honey-colored eyes and a sad face. She looked almost hollow. Her neck pale, bird-like. Her arms thin as matchsticks. She was sitting up in a queen-sized bed, reading from a black book. She uttered a cry when she saw us. She probably thought we were burglars for her eyes opened wide and her face turned stark white. She shut the book and placed it beside her, put her hands palms-up on the bedsheets.

"We just wanted to see if you really exist," I stammered.

"If you don't leave at once I will call the police," she said. Her voice was steady—after all, she was a murderess—and her lower lip quivered as if in silent rage.

I don't know what overcame me, but suddenly I felt emboldened. "People say your house is haunted," I said.

She frowned. "And you believe them?"

"That you kidnap children."

"Is that so?"

"And that you killed your husband."

"Don't believe everything you hear."

"But you did kill him, didn't you?"

Silence.

It occurred to me then that if she had killed her husband she could just as easily kill me—now—and not think twice about it. I looked at my sister; her face was white with fear.

"He died of old age," the old woman continued. "Peacefully, in his sleep. It happens that way if we are lucky."

She spoke the words calmly, without a hint of apprehension, but I noticed that her hands were trembling, and I saw upon her hands a network of tiny lines that crisscrossed her palms, lines that formed the very image of a dead man's face.

My sister said, "Let's go."

It must have been shortly thereafter when the old woman left the house in the forest. There was a rumor that she had been run out of town. Jill and I stayed away from the forest for a while. We talked of anything but the old woman. We played in the fields at the edge of town, ran barefoot through grass that was like a cloak of moss stretched out upon the earth. But in the springtime we returned to the forest. The trees were green. Wildflowers bloomed in a myriad of colors. Another rumor: this time that the old woman—or rather her ghostly silhouette—had returned to haunt the house in the forest. There was talk that the men of the town were going to burn her place to the ground so that we would be rid of her forever, but nothing came of it and the incident was eventually forgotten. Except by me and my sister. We would never forget. For we had seen her. We returned many nights thereafter to check for the light in the house, but it was never on. And I was not about to go up to the front door and knock.

ROSÉ CLARE, A LIFE

I

I traveled that day to Gungadere, a small town on the southern coast of France. I was looking for Princess Gwenedine, the most beautiful woman in all of Europe. She had haunting, gray-green eyes, the color of the sea before it storms, and golden-brown hair that fell in waves upon her shoulders. Her body was wonderfully proportioned, as if created by a master sculptor out of heavenly stone. She'd had many suitors but remained unmarried. Tales of her torrid romances traveled up and down the countryside, and more than once, news concerning her imminent betrothal was announced. But she had never wed.

Now it was my duty to arrest Gwenedine on the charge of murder. It seems her suitors were not suitors at all, but innocent victims of a heinous crime: she would win their trust, their love, would promise them her hand in marriage; then, one night, after they had made love and were sleeping peacefully, she would steal from them all their earthly possessions, plant a dagger in their breast, and throw their bodies into the sea. It was believed she was responsible for the deaths of twenty-eight men over the past several years. Gwenedine had been seen only days before, making love to a sailor on the outskirts of Gungadere. Our informant watched in silence as they made love together, as the charms of her lovemaking unfolded. And I, Chief Investigator Rosé Clare, Special Forces Homicide Division, I was to put an end to it all.

What my superiors did not know, and what I was not about to tell them, was that I had been in love with Gwenedine once before, madly, passionately, hopelessly in love. Twenty years before, when I was barely twenty-one. We met at the police academy, at the Ecole du Criminology, though I never understood why she had enrolled: she had no interest in crime or the laws that defined it; her only interest was in love and the rules that governed it—of which she claimed there were none. I remember one evening when she pulled me into her room with urgent entreaties. Her voice a sultry siren's wail. Mesmerized by her beauty, drunk with youthful love, I humbly complied. I would have said anything that night to obtain her love! She laughed for she realized I was bound to her by a magic spell. We made love until dawn, holding each other tightly, frantically, as if afraid death itself might come and tear us apart. But death did not come. Not that night, nor the nights that followed. What separated us in the end—what separates us all in the end—was the simple passing of time. Or that is what I forced myself to believe. Gwenedine simply vanished one day, without an explanation, leaving not a trace. I received from her only a postcard, weeks later, from the Rue des Rêvers in Paris. I miss you, Rosé, she wrote, and signed herself, Your beloved Gwenedine. But from that day forward not a word.

Her disappearance threw me into the blackest depression: What had I done wrong? How had I offended her? There is nothing more terrible than the end of love. Your soul aches, you do not want to go on living. Nor was Gwenedine there for me to question or confront; there was not even the ghost of her presence with which I could do battle.

How would I react when I now confronted her? Would I wilt (again) before her beauty? I did not know.

And as it turned out, I would not discover how—at least not that day. For when I reached Gungadere I found it empty, a ghost town. No sign of Gwenedine or any other living person. I shook my head. Information was not reliable in this day and age; informants were not to be believed. Gungadere looked as though it had been abandoned for eons. I had been lured there by someone for some unknown reason. Perhaps Gwenedine herself, intending to try her tricks on me, make love to her former lover amongst these ruins. Then off with his head and into the sea! Only she'd had a change of heart. Poor Rosé; today he shall be spared! she sighs. But it had probably been a prank. One of my enemies—a former criminal I put behind bars—learned of my recent assignment and managed to have me sent on this wild-goose chase. And after I spent days looking through the rubble of this decaying town—looking for what? for Gwenedine? for the corpse of our love?—and came up empty-handed, everyone would laugh. Perhaps I would even be demoted. I did not care. People were always expecting miracles of investigators. Catch the criminals quickly and lock them up forever!

A strong wind was blowing in from the sea and a thick fog was descending upon the town, blanketing it with a coat of misty gray. I turned to go. Gwenedine, murder? Never. She was no more able to murder than I was to dismiss the memory of her love.

Which I shall never do.

Gwenedine, Gwenedine, where are you? In truth, I had looked forward to meeting you again that day. To facing down ghosts from long ago. To putting them to rest forever.

II

I was seated on a park bench watching the clouds as they floated serenely by when seemingly out of nowhere, a young woman appeared and fell onto the bench beside me. She was a pretty woman—mid-twenties, I guessed—but her face was flushed and her skirt rumpled as if she had been in a fight. Fearing the worst, I tried to ask if something was wrong, but I could not get two words in edgewise. She was in a state of feverish excitement and her words would not stop.

"I am happy, oh! I am so happy," she said. "I have a new lover, you see, a kind and gentle man, and what I have hoped, dreamed, and wished for, for what has seemed centuries, has finally come to pass, to be realized as a living, breathing truth, and a life of the most abject misery—my life until now—has finally come to an end.

"In how many ways have I imagined I would meet my love: while strolling down the Rue de la Monde in Paris, it is love at first sight, our eyes meet, I see into the depths of his soul, he sees into the depths of mine; on the hot sands of the Sahara, the sun burning our bodies, our flesh throbbing with youthful love, our lips meet, his tongue tastes mine, I take his hand and he is mine; on the beach at Devil's Cove, warm salty spray fills the air, our minds have become one, our hearts one, I have never felt more at peace, our love is slow, delicious, and bountiful.

"But in the end it was much simpler: I met my love while walking home from work. An ordinary event on an ordinary day. We could not wait to reach the bed in my apartment (it was nearly a mile away) but instead hurried to an empty field that was nearby and fell upon the grass, he pulling off my clothes (wildly, like a man who is starved for love), I pulling off his, until we lay naked on the grass, mad with a love we knew to be eternal. And all the love that had been inside of me, waiting impatiently to be released, was released. And I knew at last the true meaning of fulfillment. We have met many times since, each encounter (dare I say it?) even better than the one before. And now I can say, with the utmost conviction, that everything in my life is wonderful, absolute perfection.

"Of course my lover is not real. Such a magnificent creature has never walked the Earth, nor ever will. Nor would I wish it otherwise. For if he were corporeal, if he breathed the air we do, by that very act he would become imperfect and therefore our love would become imperfect. And that I simply could not stand! My lover may not be real, but in my thoughts he is real and it is precisely this reality of his unreality that gives him substance—like a ghost that haunts the night, except he haunts my days and nights.

"This is what I like best about my lover: he comes when I call him: he comes when I wish it. He is not a particularly young man; in fact, he is a man well along in years, but he is a magnificent lover nonetheless. His hair is jet-black (black as night, black as hell) and curls around the collar. His cheekbones are high, his nose long and prominent, like a hawk's. His neck is graceful, his torso muscular and smooth. But it is his eyes, his dark-brown eyes, that hold me transfixed, I cannot take my eyes from them. They are as large as chestnuts and seem to sparkle with a light that emanates from deep within. Peering into his eyes is like peering into another world, a world where there is no time, no place, no existence as you or I know it. He always wears a black cloak with brass buttons down the middle. It makes him look demonic! And when he opens it up, I see the universe inside: the sun, the moon, and all the stars. My lover is always ready to entertain me, to do whatever I desire. But he is also always the gentleman: He takes me dancing, to the theater, and on romantic trips abroad. There is no place we cannot go. He is so kind, so gentle. And when we make love—that is kind and gentle, too, as is the sleep which follows: kind and gentle, filled with sweet dreams and peace. He bows when it is time to leave. He looks so somber as he kisses my hand. 'Until we meet again,' he says and then a smile brightens his face. I cannot suppress a giggle, I am sixteen years old again, innocent and unassuming, I have never been so happy!"

She left me then, dancing aimlessly across the park like a butterfly lost in flight. I smiled and thought to myself: Such is the nature of happiness: it does not reflect what really is; it reflects what we believe. And any belief may become a reality—provided only one has the will to believe it is so.

III

I was alone in an open field. The grass was brownish black, sere. A vulture stood before me. It was six feet tall and was gazing at me severely.

"Have mercy on me!" I cried as the bird plunged its beak deep into my neck, again and again. I had lost track long ago how many times it had thrust its beak into me. The vulture said nothing; of course, it couldn't talk. The air wheezed through my throat and my eyes inflated into two large spheres. I studied my attacker: a large bird, naked, with two monstrous wings. The vulture moved lower, pecking at my chest. Clumps of tumbleweed lay scattered on the ground. I hadn't noticed them before, but they were of no use to me—and there were no trees or bushes for escape. And yet escape was impossible because I was unable to move my legs. The only bodily appendages I did control were my arms. These I flung about wildly; I had long ago given up trying to hit the vulture and now simply swung my arms in a pathetic display of impotence. Armed resistance was out of the question: I possessed no weapons; nor did words have any effect on the vulture: it had shown no response to the vulgarities I had hurled at it throughout the day.

When a man approaches death he often realizes his life is drawing to a close, likewise I realized my end was probably near. And yet I was truly puzzled at this execution—that was what it was—and throughout the day I held steadfastly to my innocence. I looked up into a torrid, blue sky, searching for an answer to my predicament, something to give meaning to my life's final moments, but I saw only the blinding sun, directly over-head, whose rays scorched the earth.

I looked back down—the vulture was preparing another blow. "You belong to the dead, you damn bird," I cried, if for no other reason than to break the now deaf-ening silence. The vulture moved to my arms, having fin-ished with the chest. My heart had been carefully pecked around so as not to upset its beating. Surprisingly, noth-ing ached. I had given myself up for lost and was sinking into a pit of despair when suddenly the vulture stopped. I heard a sound off in the distance, and looking up, I saw a huge, black mass descending over the mountains. "Call to your friends . . ." I said, speaking with as much force as I could muster with my nearly collapsed lungs, but the words froze in midair and fell silently to the ground. Even nature was conspiring against me. The vulture smiled slyly as it studied my decrepit condition. Is it fi-nally full? I thought. Or is this the moment before it sends me to my death? My arms lay on the ground, merely tendons and a bit of rotting flesh. My throat was gone, my brain was gone, my chest was filled with holes. Hardly was I presentable to any woman. The vulture drew up to its full height, as tall as any mountain, and it pulled its giant head back. Its beak was razor sharp and its eyes glowed like two exploding suns. It will aim for my heart. I know it will not miss. But when the blow was struck it fell an inch below the heart, puncturing the rib cage for what must have been the hundredth time. "For God's sake, dispatch me at once," I moaned. The bird's response was to begin pecking at my groin. Moments lat-er it looked up and into my soul with innocent eyes that only increased the torture.

And suddenly all was clear to me, the truth emerging out of the skies like the dawn of a brand-new day: it was not my death that was intended, but my inju-ry, not the loss of my life, but of my manhood. "Stop!" I cried, half in terror at the onset of this final phase of my demise, half in disgust at the ugliness of this creature who would stoop to any low to satisfy its wormy appetite.

Much to my amazement, the vulture drew back abruptly. It hesitated a moment—perhaps my cries had touched some vestige of compassion deep within? It uttered a horrid croaking sound and sibilated uncontrollably.

And then, quite unexpectedly, it spoke:

"You have only to say so," it said. Then it flew away.

IV

"Life has impenetrable mysteries, however solvable they at first appear."

"But—" I began.

"No," Jennifer said. "Don't even try. It's hopeless."

She shut the door and I was alone on the porch. Why was she like this? Why was she so cruel? Her face so hard, so cold, so impenetrable. As if our relationship itself was hard, cold, and impenetrable. Maybe that was what she meant. Or maybe she didn't mean anything at all by what she said, maybe she merely wanted me to leave.

I started back down the road towards the city. My mind was in a fog. I was head over heels in love with this woman, with Jennifer Lambért, and I couldn't think clearly.

A car whizzed past; it was traveling well over the speed limit, though that was not unusual around here. The driver honked his horn and yelled as he flew by. I saw that he was smiling. Did I know him? Suddenly the car veered off the road and the tires squealed as they rocked over the dusty berm before the driver was able to regain control. "Watch out!" I cried, but he did not hear my words for he was far down the road. As the sound of the engine faded, I realized how quiet it was out here in the country. All I could hear were the limpid songs of the birds. The sparrows and the whippoorwills. A warbler's gentle trill. I gazed upon a gentle blue sky. In the east, puffy white clouds moved lazily towards the horizon.

Above me all was clear. I wanted to rise into the sky, to become one with the beautiful blue sky, to forget my lost love and my anguish—my anguish for my lost love. I shut my eyes and imagined my body becoming lighter. I rose on my tiptoes, as if trying to will myself into the atmosphere, but to no avail. The laws of physics are not about to change to suit the wild fancies of ordinary men. It was then that I grew dizzy; I opened my eyes and threw out my arms to keep from falling.

And I saw it.

It was a glass mirror, lying on the side of the road. Oblong in shape, about six inches wide and four inches high. Perhaps the side-view mirror from the auto that had passed me by.

I picked up the mirror and looked into the glass. And I gasped. I could not see my reflection! I was looking directly into the mirror, but I was not there. I saw only the scene behind me: an empty road, a copse of pine trees, an abandoned well. My heart was beating rapidly and my hands felt clammy. Was I hallucinating? It was possible, though I'd never been one to suffer from a false perception of events. I pinched myself. The sensation was real. I examined into the sky. The sky was real. There was the sun, a translucent sphere, showering me with rays of light. There were the clouds, light and spongy, like marshmallows. They had moved further east, but they were still there. I stamped my feet against the pavement. The road was there. The road was real. And everything around me was still.

I took a deep breath and turned my attention back to the mirror. Only it was not a mirror. It was a looking glass. A looking glass which reflected not that which was around me, but images from another place: I saw the sun in a clear blue sky, shining over a desert filled with dunes of gray sand. I saw a camel—no, a caravan of camels—in the distance and two figures in white robes leading them ahead. I had the distinct impression I was looking at a scene from long ago, centuries past. The figures continued onward, shepherding the camels across the desert and gradually faded from view. My eyes were left with only the desert itself, silent, cold, and empty. The scene dissolved and I found myself looking into a garden full of poppies, roses, and peonies. In the middle of the garden I saw a woman wearing a Roman stola. She plucked a rose and began drinking in its fragrance. She looked at me and smiled, she held out her hand. "God almighty!" I cried, but before I could say another word a young man emerged from a house adjacent to the gar-den; he took the woman in his arms and they kissed. Then they drew apart and, holding hands, moved off down a garden path that wound away from the house. The scene dissolved. And then I saw them amongst the ruins of Troy, making love amongst the ruins of that dead city.

The looking glass is telling lies, I thought. I must pay no attention.

Easier said than done. The images continued, holding me spellbound like a sorcerer's spell. At first I thought my anxiety might be due to these unsettling per-ceptions, which would have flustered the most resolute of men, but then I realized the answer was otherwise: ensuing scenes, which marched through the ages, were familiar to me, like the lines across the palms of my hands. I realized that the looking glass was replaying my own history, showing me images of my time upon the earth. And who amongst us will not look upon their past? Who amongst us will ignore their own beginning?

I looked into the mirror. I would not turn my eyes from the images I saw in the mirror. I heard the soft moans of a man and woman making love; I saw myself being born; I saw my elementary school; I saw Mrs. Mo-rell, the second-grade teacher on whom I'd had such a crush; I saw Hazel, who'd taught me what it meant to be a man (but not directly: I'd watched from behind the trees as boy after boy possessed her on a riverbank). I witnessed the dissolution of my parent's marriage; I saw their divorce; I saw my brother dying of cancer in a hos-pital ward; I saw myself seeing Jennifer Lambért for the first time on the coast of France; I saw myself writing letters of love, pleading for time; I saw myself calling her on the phone, heard her implore me to leave her alone; I saw myself going to her house, saw the door slam in my face; I saw myself walking along the road to the city; I saw a car driving past; I saw myself come upon the mirror; I saw myself looking into the mirror; I saw myself looking at myself at this very moment, looking at my other self which lay on the other side of this looking glass.

Just then I was conscious of the looking glass growing hotter. The image of the sun upon the mirror grew larger, a blinding, white light, tearing into my soul. I held onto the glass for as long as I could stand the pain, I had to see what happened next. Dimly, through the blinding light, I saw myself approaching Jennifer, she was on her knees, she was crying. A man—I could not tell who—was behind her. What did he want? Was he friend? Was he foe? Something was horribly wrong. And then I saw her turn to face him. It seemed to me that she knew him—her look was one of recognition—and I thought I saw her smile.

"No!" I cried and I thrust my hand into the mirror. Or rather, I attempted to do so. But my hand struck glass that was hot as fire and I cried out in pain. I dropped the mirror. I expected to hear glass shattering as the mirror hit the pavement, but all was silent. I looked down and saw nothing: no looking glass, no fragments of glass, and I felt as if a great weight had been lifted from my shoulders, my despair consigned to the cellar of distant memories. It was only a dream, I thought. The hallucinations of an unhappy heart. But before I had time to utter a sigh of relief it reappeared. Only it wasn't a looking glass. It was a sun. A second sun. It was the size of a saucer as it hovered at eye-height, no more than a dozen feet before me, a hellacious ball of fire. As the minutes passed, I saw that the sun was growing weaker, its rays less intense, its size shrinking, until after an hour or two—I waited that long, perhaps longer, perhaps centuries—it was gone. "Come back," I called out—I have no idea why, my hands were blistered from the heat—but the sun had vanished and once again I was alone.

When I reached the city, I made my way to a park on the outskirts of town, where I sat down on a bench and tried to ascertain the meaning of what had passed before my eyes.

* * *

I've been coming to this bench for years. To sit and reflect whenever I'm troubled or confused. And I wonder: perhaps life is but a series of visions, frames comprising a movie that can never be viewed and thus never understood. It's a sobering thought, but one which, I fear, might be true.

I'm a statue, rooted. A cardinal alights on my shoulder and I freeze. A woman draws near, camera extended. She snaps a picture and smiles. And then she asks my name.

THE TOWN THAT WENT TO SLEEP

It was a hot July day in the sleepy town of Backwater, Mississippi. Population 7,953. Miss Dawn Feathercock was sitting in the rocking chair on the front porch of her parent's stately two-story brick home. Dawn was an attractive woman with wavy red hair that flowed to her waist like a river of silk, laughing green eyes, and a capacious bosom. She was twenty-two years old and the object of affection of countless men in town but she had yet to offer her hand to any of them.

The deep-blue sky was cloudless that day. The air deathly still. Dawn was the first person to see the sporty red convertible speeding down the dusty road that ran in front of the house. "Good Lord," she cried as the unknown vehicle roared by, light-blue exhaust spewing from the tailpipes. The man at the wheel was only a blur, but even so she was certain she saw him wave at her and smile.

* * *

It was thirty minutes later, in the fading light of the afternoon, when Dawn rose from the porch, hurried up the stairs to her bedroom, put on her favorite blue dress and yellow sunbonnet, crossed the hall to the bathroom, powdered her face and arranged her hair, went back outside, across the walkway and down the dusty road that led to the center of town. Her destination was Treyborne's Grocery Store. She would purchase a side of beef, four medium potatoes, eight white onions, a few carrots, and a bunch of parsley for the evening meal. Louisiana Stew. Her parents' favorite.

* * *

Dawn saw Farmer Brown working in his fields on the edge of town and she waved. He stopped, wiped the perspiration from his brow, and gave her a grin. Farmer Brown was a corpulent man with a thick neck and lumberjack arms. He was known throughout town as a man of strong character and good humor, even if he was eccentric. Today, he looked like an overstuffed teddy bear with his blue overalls, red cotton shirt, and high black boots. She giggled. She had always loved Farmer Brown.

He motioned her to him. She frowned and pointed at her dress. She would get it dirty if she trudged across the field, she cried out. He laughed and came over to her. "Where you headed?" he asked.

"To town."

He smiled. "To see that preacher man, I bet."

"Who?"

"Herbert Horatio Stent. The man from Tupelo. Running for Head of the Glorified Unification Church of the One True Righteous God. Least that's what he says. Don't know what he thinks he can accomplish here though. We're all atheists, aren't we?" He winked.

Dawn shook her head. "I'm off to the grocery. It's father's birthday and I want to cook him something special."

Farmer Brown nodded. "Good girl. I always said you had your priorities straight."

He clapped her on the back and then he turned and headed back into the fields.

Dawn walked on in the slanting afternoon sun. She heard birds chirping from a nearby tree. A mangy gray dog barked at her from the side of the road. She had never seen the animal before and he didn't look too friendly. She quickened her step. Cumulus clouds had moved in from the west, but they did nothing to hide the burning sun. Dawn had never known it to be so hot. Like an inferno, she thought. She looked at the flowers on the hillside that overlooked Farmer Brown's fields. Pale-blue flowers with golden-yellow centers. What were they called? Bluebells? Blueangels? No—bluets, that was it. Or something like that. She could never remember. They must have been hardy to withstand the sultry summer heat. Next time she saw Farmer Brown she would be sure to ask their name.

She passed Dottie Flanigan's house and she saw her looking out the living room window. Dot was a rambunctious woman with raven hair and milky-white skin. Dawn waved and Dot waved back. Seconds later the front door opened and Dot emerged onto the porch.

"Watcha doin'?"

"Heading to town. Need anything?"

"No, I don't think so." Dottie paused. "Though if you see the preacher tell him I'm sorry I missed yesterday's sermon."

"Preacher Stent?"

"There's none other in Backwater, is there?"

"None that I know of. When did he arrive?"

"Three weeks ago. Where have you been? He's all people are talking about! You've holed yourself up in your house, Dawn. Readin' too many books. Is that all you ever do?"

"Course not."

"I guess then it's just that you don't believe."

Dawn frowned. "Nobody does, do they?"

"Not true!" Dot shot back. "Well, maybe at first they didn't. Herb was jeered—you're right. But only for a little while. After people got to talking things over they changed their way of thinking."

"Is that so?"

"You go hear him now; you'll see."

It was then Dawn noticed that Dot was holding an oversized, black book in her left hand. She had never known her friend to read much and she asked what it was.

"The Bible, silly." Dot laughed. "Herb passes them out. You of all people should recognize it. Now you better get going or you'll be late."

* * *

Dawn was approaching the center of town when she heard a rumble that sounded like distant thunder. She wondered what it might be. Another block and then she heard clapping and cheering. Her heart skipped a beat when she rounded the final corner and saw a crowd gathered in the park across from the grocery. Everyone was gazing at a middle-aged man wearing a gray seersucker suit and dark necktie who was standing before a wooden dais. The platform stood atop a stage papered with red, white, and blue bunting. There was a banner hanging in front which read: "Reverend Herb Stent: Backwater's Choice."

Dawn drew closer. There must have been at least five hundred people assembled. Why, she had never seen such a crowd in Backwater! The preacher's eyes shifted from one person to the other as he took them all in. He pulled a silk handkerchief from his shirt pocket and wiped it across his deeply furrowed brow.

Dawn tapped the back of the lady in front of her and asked, "What's going on?"

The lady turned and Dawn beheld an elderly woman with a thin face and dark-brown eyes. "Herb's remarkable, isn't he?" the woman said. "The best preacher in Mississippi. He's got my vote!"

Religion was not a favorite topic in Backwater. The clergy had ignored the place for years and with good reason. Ever since the war, which had claimed four of Backwater's young men, belief in a higher deity faded. No one found it within their heart to forgive God for what had happened. Not a single person attended church one year which meant the collection plates had gone empty. The town's leading church disbanded when it became apparent the south's religious leaders had no desire to pay attention to Backwater any longer. The remaining churches followed suit, and the town soon became known as a home for atheists.

Now something had changed. But what?

Herb Stent was a charismatic man with languorous dark-brown eyes. His voice a booming baritone that shattered the stillness of the park. Dawn could see why Dot found him attractive.

He grinned maniacally as he pointed at the crowd. "You are going to sleep!" he cried. "Every one of you!"

Dawn moved away. She'd always felt awkward in crowds.

* * *

Herb became the talk of the town. In coffee shops, barber shops, Ramsey Park, all over Backwater, everyone had their opinion. Many thought him charming and found themselves wooed by his seductive words. Others wondered aloud at his motive—what was he doing in Backwater, anyway? A reporter from the local newspaper investigated Herb's background and concluded it was just as Farmer Brown had said: Herb was running for head of the Glorified Unification Church of the One True Righteous God. The church was the brainchild of the well-known pastor Richard Stent the Third, the preacher's father. It had grown by leaps and bounds over the past decade, mainly in the south, where it had arisen in the Mississippi delta region, but its influence was beginning to spread north as well—having recently reached the suburbs of Washington D.C.

* * *

"Did you hear?"

"What?"

"Fast asleep."

"Who?"

"Old Miss Watercress. Keeled over at dinner last night. Slumped in her chair like a dead woman and began to snore."

"Sick?"

"Don't believe so."

"She's old. How old is she? She must be in her nineties."

"She's eighty-two. Or thereabouts. Healthy as a horse and always has been. I doubt anything's wrong with her, if that's what you're thinking."

"Nothing the doctors could detect. But it happened a week ago and she still hasn't woken."

* * *

It began, not surprisingly, in the old people's home on the edge of town. One by one residents began sleeping for periods much longer than normal, sixteen, twenty hours, sometimes for days at a time. Usually it happened suddenly, the affected persons dropping to the floor in apoplectic fits that turned into a maddening silence as they lost consciousness. In other cases it was like a fog which smothered the afflicted, as if they were drowning in molasses. Soon people all over town were complaining of feeling "not quite there."

And they weren't.

The town's doctors were puzzled. One diagnosed it as collective amnesia; loss of memory seemed to be a complicating factor and would linger for weeks after the initial episode. Another thought it related to African sleeping sickness, a malady known to affect countries of that continent and which may have been brought to the state by an unsuspecting visitor, perhaps a visiting professor at the University of Mississippi. Reverend Stent, solemnly pontificating, said it was something else entirely; the citizens of Backwater were the chosen ones, the true believers. Soldiers falling in line.

* * *

In Ramsey Park, Herb was speaking. He had been in Backwater nearly a month and the citizenry talked of no one else. The local newspaper ran a series of editorials praising his positions. And though the election was a month away, they had already given him their unqualified endorsement. No one knew the names of those running against Herb. Indeed, no one knew if anyone was running against him. It was as if a hurricane was blowing through town, as if a great flood was washing everything away, as if time itself had stopped.

Herb went on for nearly an hour on the state of religion in Mississippi, the issues that affected the populace—issues of decadence and sin—and by all accounts his sermon was thought-provoking. Some found his words profound and were swayed by his reasoning. Others weren't so sure. Parts made sense, they admitted, but other parts seemed like pure babble. Still others were convinced the man was a charlatan, a nincompoop, a fool.

* * *

"It's a rotten shame, you know."
"What do you mean?"
"The man's a fake. Any fool can see that."
"Some think him a saint."
"His eyes are shifty."
"Or an angel."
"He has no wings."
"You don't need wings to speak the word of God."

"Did you see that scar across his left cheek? His alien eyes? Marks of the devil, I tell you! He wants something and he takes us for fools."

* * *

Dawn's father, former pastor of the now defunct Church of the Holy Cross, was one of those who considered Herb a heathen. "He's after something," he said one day. "I just don't know what."

"Some people says he's the son of God," Dawn said.

"It doesn't matter what anyone says," her father insisted. "The man's a blasphemer."

Dawn fidgeted, afraid to say what she knew was on both of their minds.

* * *

It was no longer confined to the elderly. All over town people of all ages were succumbing to an endless sleep. The newspaper termed it an epidemic of biblical proportions. The town's doctors were pursuing promising leads but had yet to come up with a definitive cause. A cure was months if not years away, they said. And that meant time was running out.

* * *

It was ten o'clock one morning the first week of September when Dawn found Farmer Brown in his fields, tilling the land. The sky was a serene blue. A pair of red hawks glided overhead.

"Let me tell you about Herb," Farmer Brown said and he drew so close that Dawn could feel his soft breath against her cheek as he whispered into her ear, "He's an angel." Startled, she stepped back. "An angel from Heaven. Sent here by the Lord to cure us of our ills. But you know what? The people in Backwater aren't wise enough to understand his words. Nope, not a one. He's tried; oh, has he tried! Sermonizing to the masses for hours on end, but his words have fallen on deaf ears. People think they know what he's saying, mind you. But have you noticed that everyone has their own interpretation? And not one of them is right, not one!"

"Dottie says Herb is the wisest man she's ever listened to."

"Most likely he is."

"And that when he speaks of the human race he's really talking about the people of Backwater."

"Certainly."

"And that he will waken us to the evils that surround us."

"Right again."

Dawn coughed to clear her throat. "But what he's really doing is murdering us, isn't he?"

Farmer Brown looked deep into her emerald eyes. She seemed terribly sad. "It may be—as Herb says—that we live in a land of infidels. I don't know. But I'm not sure it matters and I know that I don't care. Not anymore." He reached out to touch Dawn's cheek, her soft alabaster cheek upon which tears were slowly falling.

* * *

Dawn wasn't sure what to make of what Farmer Brown had told her. She wanted to keep talking, but he had turned and was heading back into the fields.

She headed home, walking slowly down the dusty road. In her mind, she saw the brilliant light of an explosion, clouds of black smoke, orange flames shooting skyward. It was if she was suspended in a dream.

She remembered Farmer Brown telling her once that if anything should happen to him he wanted her to watch over the farm. How could she do that? A young woman of twenty-two. Perhaps he meant for her to watch over the flowers that bloomed on the hillside. Those pretty blue flowers that smelled so heavenly. And that she would be sure to do.

* * *

The next day she found Herb Stent in the trailer park on the edge of town. He was washing his red convertible, rubbing it down with a shiny black cloth. A mangy gray dog was sleeping on the grass beside him, and it raised its ear as she approached.

It was late afternoon, the air thick, the heat stifling. She took a deep breath, screwed up her courage.

"Reverend Stent, what are you doing here?"

He looked up, startled, then smiled when he saw her. Another soul to save, he thought. There were so many. "Why do you ask, my dear?" he said.

"Farmer Brown says you are an impostor."

"And you believe him?"

"Truly, sir, I don't know what to believe."

"That's why I am here. To tell you."

"But I don't know whether to believe you or not."

"You must. You must believe."

"What if you're a liar, an impostor? Reverend Stent, what if you're the Antichrist?"

"But that isn't true. I care simply about the salvation of the soul."

"Mine or yours?"

He scrutinized her with cold, punctilious eyes, and his lips curled into an odd, twisted smile. "Your tongue is tart, my child. That will not serve you."

There was poison in that voice, she thought.

"Your problem is that you are so young," he continued. "You haven't had time to lose your faith."

"I have no faith to lose," she answered. "Not anymore."

* * *

Three days later, Farmer Brown was found dead, his body hanging from the bough of an oak tree. He had been harassing young girls, it was said. The police were making inquiries. Dawn could not believe what was happening and she ran to his farm on the edge of town where she knew he must have been, imagined his body dangling from the bough of an oak tree, swinging slowly in a breeze that came in from the south, the fresh aroma of blueberries pouring down from the hillside. Suddenly she felt a terrible vertigo. Her head was heavy as lead and her eyelids were closing and everything was misty and she lay on the grass and soon she was fast asleep, slip, slipping away into an endless dream.

* * *

Herb Stent, itinerant preacher, blue-eyed son of one of the most famous preachers in the south, Richard Stent the Third, founder of the Glorified Unification Church of the One True Righteous God, was in the town square, waiting for an audience that would never come, for the collective heartbeats of Backwater had been stilled.

When another hour passed and the park was still empty, he realized what had happened. And he knew that with the town asleep he would get no votes. He would never succeed his father as head of the Glorified Unification Church which was what he wanted more than anything else on this earth. "What an imbecile I am," he muttered. "I've only been wasting my time in this place."

He scowled and spat on the ground in disgust. He wiped a hand across a weary brow. He got into his sporty red convertible and drove away.

A SOLDIER'S LAMENT

Her back against the cold stone wall, the village girl looked at the firing squad with terrified eyes. It seemed impossible, but her life had reached its end. She breathed slowly, steadily, trying with all her power to remain calm. The one thing she could not do—even if she were about to die—was admit to them that she was terrified. She still had her dignity and she intended to keep that until her death. Death. She shuddered at the thought. Death itself was not what scared her; but why, oh why, did it have to end this way?

Raul approached—trembling visibly—and he looked her in the eye. He wanted to speak but he just stood there with his hands limply at his sides. An awkward silence that seemed to last for an eternity. And then a member of the firing squad stepped forward impatiently, and without even looking at Raul, he put the blindfold on the girl. The silver epaulets on his uniform were like a badge of courage, but to the village girl he was a man without honor. Silence. She heard only the sounds of birds in the distance, chattering on oblivious to the drama unfolding below. At that moment, as her thoughts began to wander, she was jolted back to reality. It was not what she expected: with almost painful precision she felt the kiss of death upon her cheek and her mind giving way as it was absorbed back into the cosmos. It was a wonderful feeling and she did not attempt to fight it. She welcomed it, rather, as a weary traveler welcomes the fall of the anodynic night. She grew calm and her body still as memory drained away.

"Fire!" And when the bullets pierced her chest, when her angel's blood began to flow onto the ground, she was already dead. The bullets did not harm her.

It was then that Raul realized the commanding officer was at his side. "The chief insurgent's daughter," the man said matter-of-factly. "Helena, wasn't that her name?"

"Helen."

"Should have been Helena. Sounds more feminine. Then she probably would never have gotten mixed up in this revolutionary business. She would have been too busy being some soldier's whore."

"I don't know, sir." Raul looked sullen, as if he had just lost a close friend.

His commander paused and tapped his boots against the ground, trying to shake free the red clay that stubbornly clung to the soles. Then he said, "You loved her, didn't you?"

"My feelings are of no concern, sir."

The commander grimaced. "No concern! I gave the order for the execution to be carried out precisely at sunrise, at 6:04 this morning. Did you hear me, soldier? This morning at 6:04! Do you know what time it is? 3:15 in the afternoon! If the firing squad hadn't decided to carry out the execution on its own, who knows how long this would have dragged on. What have you been doing the past nine hours?"

"She had a last wish, sir. She wanted a few moments, sir, to collect her thoughts. How could I deny that, sir. That was all she wanted."

"A wish that lasted for nine hours?!"

"I didn't realize so much time had passed."

"Like hell you didn't, soldier. You couldn't bring yourself to kill her because you were in love with her, isn't that true? You let your emotions interfere with your work. I could have you shot for this."

"Yes, sir."

Even now, Raul was not sure how it had happened. He had sworn off politics. He promised his family he would do so and he had meant to keep his word. But the infinite war raged on and one day the enemy overran their village, raped the women, feasted on meat from the village stores, and ordered all men over the age of twenty to enlist. Raul had done so only because he did not care anymore. He was tired of the propaganda that was everywhere, the lies and the half-truths. But then this serpentine girl came along and he fell in love with her, the first woman he had ever loved, and as luck would have it, she had been a member of the opposition. When she was caught and someone in his regiment informed against him, he was ordered to carry out her execution. Disobeying the commander's orders had been the easiest decision of his life.

The commander scowled. "Well?"

"If one side doesn't get you, the other side will," Raul said resignedly.

The commanding officer eyed Raul coolly as if deciding whether it was worth continuing the conversation. Raul looked like a man of stone, unmoved by the entire affair. He did not seem to understand the meaning of his actions! And that bothered the commanding officer. Where there was no obedience to the law there was anarchy. And that meant the commanding officer was losing control. He grit his teeth, grabbed Raul's shoulders with his huge battle-scarred hands, and shouted in his face:

"There's one more thing you need to know: She was a dog. A filthy cur. Like all the other revolutionaries in this bloody country."

"Yes, sir."

"Yet you loved her. Why?—Never mind, don't answer that. I don't care. I don't care about anything that goes on in this Godforsaken place."

Raul tensed. He could not let the commander's words go unanswered. "But she wasn't like that, sir!" he cried. "She loved her country. She wouldn't harm any-one. Her only crime was that she was the daughter of—"

"Of the fucking leader of the opposition. And if that's not enough to condemn one to death, I don't know what is."

Raul realized he was wasting his breath. "Yes," he said.

"Yes, sir," the commander rebuked. "And now I want you to take your gun and go over to the prisoner and I want you to shoot her."

Raul recoiled in horror. "She's already dead."

"Sir!"

"She's already dead, sir."

"That's an order, soldier."

"I can't do it, sir."

"You will do it because it is your duty to carry out my orders without question. Do you understand?"

"I don't question them, sir. But I can't carry out this order. I am sorry. Do what you want with me."

"You don't understand, soldier. You have no choice."

Raul opened his eyes wide in astonishment. "But I do, sir—have a choice, sir. I'm not a pawn."

"That's exactly what you are! A pawn—"

"I have a choice, sir. And to prove to you that I have a choice I will right now before your very eyes make my choice: I refuse to carry out your order, sir."

"What are you talking about? Are you mad?"

Raul said nothing. His eyes looked vacant, like the eyes of a ghost. He wished he was dreaming and would wake up realizing it had been so and she would be beside him. But he knew this was not to be. He was slip, slip, slipping into another world, a world where the laws of nature as he knew them did not apply, where there was no difference between the living and the dead.

"Tell me," continued the commander, drawing back a step and speaking softly as if he were talking to a child, "was she a good lay?"

Raul bit his lip and looked away, trying to control the rage that was building within his breast. "I prefer not to answer that question, sir," he said.

The commanding officer would not be put off: "I must insist. You know what I'm asking. Was she good in bed? A good woman. Wild, like a whore. She certainly was beautiful! I bet the two of you spent many nights together fucking your brains out. . . ."

"Never, sir."

The commander shook his head. In all the time he had spent commanding this battalion he had never understood Raul Faith. This soldier was a real son of a bitch. But, even so, he never thought the man would go off half crazy. Didn't he realize they were in this war together? Didn't he know what that meant? That there were choices in life one had to make, awful choices, terrible choices, choices that civilized men in civilized times would recoil at making, but that in times of discord simply had to be made. For the good of society. For the preservation of society. Or else the whole damn country would go to hell in a handbasket and then where would they be? Who told him life was fair? It wasn't. One had to do not what one wished but what had to be done. What one was told to do. And those who did not realize that were the first to go. Like this crazy soldier.

The commander pulled out his pistol and pointed it at Raul. "Now."

"Go to hell."

The commander aimed the gun at Raul's leg and fired. Raul uttered a cry and fell to the ground, whimpering loudly. The commander spun around and barked his orders to two uniformed men who had watched the entire scene with an air bordering on indifference. "Take him away," he said.

The commander sighed. He looked at the village girl, dead. He looked at Raul, wailing away like an infant. There was blood on the ground where he had fallen and a thin trail of blood up to where the men were dragging him through the dust like a dog. The commander put his pistol in his belt. He shook his head and then he walked away.

RICHARD COURT: THE PRIEST, THE SINNER

I completed a novel the other day, a rather long novel, 963 pages to be exact, a sprawling landscape of a work, proleptically entitled *Richard Court: The Priest, The Sinner*, a novel filled with wondrous adventures, love, romance, intrigue, murder, revenge; subplots and sub-subplots; lively characterization, witty dialogue, one hundred pages of richly textured allegory; an emotionally intense central section; a suspenseful climax; and a chilling denouement. But last night, a cold October night I shall never forget, I cast the entire manuscript into the fire and now I will content myself with these few pages. I fear modern readers no longer have the patience to wade through long novels. This is the age of the supersonic; speed is everything in the modern world; the distance between a and b is no longer c but $c/2$.

Rachel Melody, the femme fatale of my novel, was a beautiful woman: mid-twenties, windswept curves, light-brown hair, chestnut eyes. She was soft-spoken, intelligent, had graduated *summa cum laude* from college and wanted nothing more than to be a writer of children's books. She was also a lady of the evening. It was a job she had taken to support her writing interests, which so far had met with little success.

One day Rachel's church received a new priest. His name was Richard Court. A handsome man, still in the flower of youth, his face unblemished, his eyes innocent, he was the talk of social circles, especially among the ladies, whose murmured confabulations revealed plots to steer Richard from the Path of Righteousness and onto the Path of Delicious Sin.

Richard was known everywhere for his moralistic views. His sermons invariably preached the importance of the family and of love. "For without love we are nothing and we cannot overcome the slightest hardships," he was often heard to proclaim. (Richard's first Christmas Mass; pages 74-78; the remark was also repeated at Sunday sermons; pages 116-118, 202-210, and 256-259.) Many people thought Richard was more than a simple priest and some thought he was a saint.

It was Richard's habit to take evening walks through town, observing the village and its people. He was a student of human nature, as are most priests. The people were a good lot, he observed, the vast majority being honest, law-abiding, and possessing the highest moral standards. (Richard at the Good Samaritan's Club; pages 123-126; incidents of the lost wallet and the misplaced handkerchief; pages 108 and 157; also the annual May Day festival; pages 150-172.)

But there were exceptions. Now and again Richard heard confessions from men he knew to be good family men, how they lusted after Rachel, how they salivated when they saw her in the streets, how they imagined it was her they faced when dining with their wives, and how, on Saturday nights when their wives were playing bingo at the town church, they were plunking down good money to spend an hour or two in Rachel's bed. Richard's wanderings sometimes took him past the Gentleman's Retreat, the town brothel and employer of the lovely Rachel. He would gaze up at the place and wonder what evils lurked within, what powers Rachel must have possessed to turn good men to sin. Over the years Richard became intrigued by confessions concerning the lady and one day he stole into the brothel, disguised as a mendicant, and plunked down fifty dollars for a session with her.

What he saw when he entered her room can only be described as a scene of overwhelming prodigality: The Elizabethan-style bed covered with satin sheets, its pillows stuffed with peacock feathers; the Oriental massage table upholstered with English leather; the porcelain sauna from which steam was slowly rising; the ornate mirrors on the ceiling and walls; and what must have been the world's most lavish collection of sexual paraphernalia—all far more excessive than any of the ceremonial extravagances found in Roman Catholicism.

But all of that was lost on Richard. His attention was riveted on the wondrous beauty who stood before him, clothed in a purple kimono that simply begged to be removed. Dazzled by her beauty, her majestic smile, her face like the Madonna's, Richard fell instantly in love. Light filled the room and he heard the voices of angels. Rachel's skin was white as alabaster, smooth as glass. Richard trembled as he touched her. How like a religious deity she was!

Now Rachel realized this was no ordinary customer, but a Holy Priest of the Highest Order, the priest Richard in fact. She had heard much about him (the article in the town paper announcing Richard's arrival; pages 20-25; various conversations overheard in the streets and at church; pages 45, 60, 102 to name but a few) and she felt heretofore unknown emotions surging within. But as is so often the case in human affairs, the heart realized what the mind would not admit and she treated him no differently than any other.

We have come to the novel's 262nd page. The next two hundred pages were packed with adventures galore, as Richard the Seminarian pursued Rachel the Beautiful, up and down the Tower of Pisa, across the Mediterranean Sea, over the steppes of Central Asia, past the Money Houses of Shanghai, and deep into that city's Palaces of Sin. Rachel was charmed by the attentions of this charming priest and gradually found herself falling in love. But she loved in silence and in fear, harboring secrets from her past. (Rachel's "O woe is me!" speech; pages 305-307; it revealed no specifics and was included to heighten suspense.)

One might think Richard was torn between loving God and loving Rachel, but no such problem arose. As he himself said, "I will give to God what is God's and to Rachel what is Rachel's." (Richard confessing to the diocesan bishop; page 392.) Also this, "To God, I give my love; and to Rachel, I give my love. For without love we are nothing and we cannot overcome the slightest hardships." (Richard soliloquizing; page 458.)

The next two hundred pages were written in French and described in minute detail the inner workings of the brothel. I proved by a dizzy pullulation of Human Themes that the Brothel is a microcosm of the World-At-Large, that the lives of men and women of today are nothing but endless repetitions of the sordid and licentious lives of those of past generations.

The concluding section (three-hundred-odd pages) commenced with Richard confessing to the bishop that he wanted to marry Rachel. The bishop, a man who always looked as though he was about to burst into tears, sighed deeply. "First you must know the truth," he said. He told Richard that Rachel was not the woman she appeared to be. She had, in fact, fabricated her own history: she had never been to college had never even learned how to write, was a full-time prostitute not a part-time one. Her early years were even more chilling: She had been taken from her family at the age of thirteen by a heartless drug dealer from Greece who sold high quality opium at exorbitant prices to the rich; she had been beaten, raped, verbally abused, and dumped on the black market where she traveled the world over and was sold for the night to any man who would pay for her. She served at the pleasure of several heads of state—and was the cause of more than one divorce—ending up years later at his town brothel, a gift of one of the town's founders. But every night, after the last customer had had his pleasure, she wept at her plight and dreamed of a savior who would carry her off to a faraway place and stay by her side forever.

Richard could not believe the bishop's words. "And how do you know all this?" he asked.

"The scandals were scandalous. They reached the highest echelons of several governments. I'm surprised you never heard. . . ."

Hearing this, Richard broke down and wept. Oh, how cruel was the world of man! He rushed from the church and did not stop until he reached the brothel; he burst inside, broke down Rachel's door, shooed away her latest customer, fell upon his hands and knees, and proposed marriage. His hair disheveled, his clothes tattered and wet (it had been raining for days and he had slipped and fallen on the brothel grounds), the sight of poor Richard would have moved the most hardened of criminals.

For a moment Rachel was silent. She looked Richard over, from head to toe, carefully weighing his words and her reply. And then came her answer:

"No."

The novel then became a psychological study. Rachel cannot love Richard because Rachel cannot love. She wanted to accept Richard's offer, and love him openly, but she had prostituted herself for so long that she no longer possessed the ability to love. She berated herself for forty-eight hours, pulling at her hair and tearing at her flesh. Then she resumed her former life. But the magic in her lovemaking was gone and soon she fell into disfavor among the townsmen. She became a common street whore whom no one wanted; then a petty thief. Eventually she committed suicide.

When Richard (who had turned his attentions back to the priesthood after Rachel refused him) received word of her death he, too, did himself in, but only after setting fire to the brothel, killing all inside. He must sin before dying, he reasoned, this to be certain he would join Rachel in hell. The novel concluded with an impassioned plea for a new Age of Reason, one based on a sincere understanding of basic Human Passions, on Friendship, Trust, Compassion, Empathy, on the highest Altruistic Principles, but above all on Love. For without love we are nothing and we cannot overcome the slightest hardships.

A story of Love. That is what my novel, now ashes, once purported to be.

PERFECT

All my life I have strived to be perfect. Every minute of every waking hour. Not that this is something so very remarkable in and of itself; countless others have tried, with varying degrees of success, to achieve perfection in their lives. Some have been content to seek perfection in a single event, such as a perfect meal or the construction of a perfect garden; others, a bit more ambitious, have sought to obtain perfection in a particular facet of their life, such as their marriage (the perfect spouse) or their career (the perfect employer). And then there are those, like me, who have sought perfection in *every* facet of their life. Of course, the failed attempts have greatly outnumbered the successful ones, with the greatest number of successes coming from the first category, only a few from the second, and none at all from the third.

Until I, like an unyielding mountain climber, scaled a mountain of despair and broken dreams, fervent hopes and false promises, to reach the dizzying heights of perfection on which I now find myself. And it is precisely this knowledge of my own perfection that brings a wondrous ecstasy to the passing of every moment. I write: "The man looked out the window," and even as the words flow onto the page the sentence is perfect. I toss a ball into the air and it makes a perfect arc. Even when I walk my gait is perfect.

But my journey has not been easy; the road to perfection is treacherous, false turns abound. Add to that the dangers created by the monsters of doom who are known to inhabit the road and you'll see why most people do not attempt the journey. That I did, and was successful, is simply a testament to my own perfection. Not that I never took a false turn or didn't come close to the edge of a precipice—I did. You see, I have not always been perfect. . . .

As a child I was bright-eyed and bushy-tailed, full of life and boyish enthusiasm, intensely curious. The words "perfection" and "imperfection" had no special meaning for me. I *knew* what they meant but beyond that I simply did not care. Nothing was "perfect" or "imperfect"; everything simply was. I went happily about the business of learning about life, disregarding any deeper interpretation I might have given the day's events.

But all that changed on a cool October day, leaves falling all around, when I was in the eighth year of my life. I was traveling in the back seat of my parent's car, my father at the wheel, my mother in the front passenger seat. We stopped at a light; pedestrians began to make their way in front of us. My mother was talking to my father about something or other, and though he pretended to listen, his eyes were fixed on a young woman who had started across the street. My father watched as she crossed in front of our car and fell laughing into the arms of a young man on the other side. The man kissed her on the cheek, twirled her around, then whisked her away. It was at that moment I saw my father sigh and a deep sadness filled his eyes and I realized that in his heart he had already been unfaithful to my mother. *I realized he was not perfect.* But I realized even more, for I saw that the episode was lost on my mother, she being too absorbed in her own conversation to notice my father's behavior. This lack of perspicacity, though less of an offense, was just as indicting. *My mother was not perfect either.*

You may quite rightly ask why it took me so long to realize that my parents were not perfect. What can I say? Youth is naive. But it is the lesson I learned that will amaze you: I did not—as one might have expected—become depressed or alarmed when I realized my parents, whom I had always held in the highest regard, were not perfect. No, my reaction was more inwardly directed. I realized that since I was the offspring of imperfect beings, I, too, was imperfect. And that I simply could not stand! I resolved then and there to do whatever was necessary to ameliorate my imperfections, quietly (I did not want others to accuse me of conceit), carefully (there could be no mistakes), and with great determination.

My first attempts took place at school. There I was constantly judged; there *my degree of imperfection was measured*. I studied incessantly; I shunned all social events. I was not, however, shunned by others. On the contrary, I was admired. My classmates marveled at my dedication, were so inspired, in fact, that they redoubled their efforts in the pursuit of their own, albeit simpler, goals.

I recall an event that occurred on the playground, when I was in elementary school, and that for me defines my early years. I had gotten into an argument with another boy who was a friend of mine. I no longer remember what the disagreement was about, but I do remember he was most upset and that he struck me across the face in anger. I raised not an arm to defend myself and this only infuriated him further. You see, to have done anything in my defense would have been to admit he was harming me, that I was *capable* of being harmed, that is, that I was not *perfect*. The incident ended with the boy bursting into tears and running away.

Several years later—I was in the eighth grade—an event occurred which was to abruptly change the course of my life. Every day at lunch a group of students—I was among them—gathered to play tetherball. As you might guess, it was my object to establish mastery of this game by winning the first game I played and every game thereafter. Unfortunately, I was never able to do so (I would usually win two or three games before losing). But the event which occurred on this day had nothing to do with winning or losing. I had just won my second game and was serving for game number three. I no longer remember who my opponent was, but I do remember that it was a close game, with the momentum shifting from one side to the other and that at one point my opponent got the upper hand and began wrapping the ball cleanly around the pole. I made a desperate stab at the ball, got caught up in my feet, and stumbled backwards into the crowd that had gathered around us. Instinctively, I reached out to break my fall—reaching for whatever I could hold onto. This turned out to be a breast of one of the more developed girls in the eighth-grade class. She jumped back, startled—and broke into a grin. "Sorry," I said. I blushed and she blushed and I continued blushing. I had discovered the nature of sexual arousal. My life would never be the same.

The years that followed were not time spent searching for the perfect woman to complement my own perfection. How I wished it were so! However, I had to be certain a woman was perfect before I would issue an invitation; for to issue an invitation to an imperfect woman would have been a sign of my own imperfection. I could tell at a glance if a woman's hair was not the right shade of brown (it had to be brown; my own, perfect, hair was brown), her laugh too harsh, her complexion too plain, her knees too knobby. I was always finding fault and, therefore, I got nowhere with the opposite sex. By age seventeen I was a lonely young man, a lonely young man yearning for affection.

Thank God, it was not to be forever!

I came upon the woman of my dreams on a cold, crisp September day in my freshman year at college. I realized at once I wanted to spend every moment at her side. She was so beautiful I trembled whenever I thought of her. She was witty, charming, intelligent, graceful. In a word, *perfect*. I followed her everywhere she went; I discovered her likes and dislikes, what perfume she wore, what authors she preferred (Jules Verne was a favorite). Once I caught her skinny dipping in a local pond. I thought of seizing the moment and proclaiming my love then and there, but I realized it was not yet time.

I decided it best to take a more subtle approach. It so happens my beloved was a member of our dormitory cooking group. I signed up, too. I was hoping that a joint culinary assignment might give me an opportunity to express my love.

I'll say flat out that from the start my beloved acted rather cool towards me. Not that I expected her to throw herself at my feet. But not once did she laugh at my jokes, comment on my magnificent physical appearance, or marvel at my discourses on the state of the world, which I was fond of delivering after a meal. Why, once I even caught her rolling her eyes after a statement I made!

One evening I decided I could wait no longer. We had been assigned dish washing duty and I was fumbling with the dishes, trying to decide how best to bring up the matter of my love. At one point she made a comment about how my feet "pointed at a peculiar angle." My first instinct was to reply that this resulted in the optimum position for cleaning dishes, but instead I decided that this was the moment to express my love. I dropped to my knees, took one of her hands in mine, and proposed marriage. Imagine my shock when I found myself rebuffed:

"I want nothing to do with you," she said. "You are nothing but an egotist. And I don't like egotists."

She threw her dish towel into the sink with disgust and left the room.

As it turned out, my grief was doubly compounded. Not only had I been scorned, but my beloved began taking up with every Tom, Dick, or Harry who came her way. My love for her became an obsession. How could she have rejected me—me, the perfect man? No, I reasoned, I had not been rejected. That was simply not within the realm of possibility. She was merely being cautious, trying to ascertain the dimensions of my love. And for that I could hardly blame her. In fact, it made me desire her even more.

Yes, you say, but what about all those other men? If she truly loved you, and was merely testing your love, she would never go to such extremes.

A good point and one I had already taken up. It became necessary to ascertain her true feelings towards these amorists. I sent her letters, asking questions, each of which was phrased in a casual, non-threatening way. I received not a single response. Instead of giving up, I redoubled my efforts; my letters took on a harder, shriller tone; still, no reply. My next series of letters demanded an explanation. These letters were returned unopened.

I became incensed. I went to her room to question her directly but was turned away at the door by a man I knew to be an imbecile. I said as much and straight to his face, but as the door was slammed shut I distinctly heard her giggle.

I seemed to see her everywhere now, laughing gayly, always with some new boyfriend on her arm. At the movies, at the library, at the grocery store, everywhere I went, there she was, with another—*imperfect*—man—a man of lesser stature, a man whose sole purpose in life was to torture me.

One day I went to the school counselor to tell him my troubles. I was told the counselor was busy with another student, but if I would please be seated he would see me shortly. I did, but he did not. *Nearly an hour* passed before the door to his office opened. And who should emerge but my beloved, laughing like some prepubescent schoolgirl, her skirt rumpled, her blouse unbuttoned. I watched in horror as a hairy arm emerged from the counselor's office and patted her gently on her behind. And then—if you can believe it—she twirled around and blew him a kiss. A kiss for all to see!

What could I do? Where could I turn for help? I found myself questioning the very foundation of our relationship. Perhaps she was not what I had taken her to be. *Perhaps she was not perfect!* How else to explain her behavior towards me? Not that I believed for a moment that she was far from attaining immortal status. Undoubtably some minor imperfection prevented her from becoming involved with me. I tried getting close to her girlfriends to learn what the problem might be. But even they would have nothing to do with me.

As the semester drew to a close, I prepared for the final showdown. I would confront my love directly; I would force an explanation from her lips. But, as she had been doing for months, she was able to elude my grasp once more: the day before my last final, she flew off to Europe. She was to be an exchange student the following semester, the Registrar's Office told me. I did not believe that for an instant.

I sold my schoolbooks, emptied my saving's account, bought a plane ticket, and flew off in pursuit. I was delirious with the fever of my love.

I traced her to the palace of a prince in Portugal, the dungeon of a duke in Denmark, the castle of a count in Constantinople, and the bastille of a baron in Barcelona. But she always managed to slip away unnoticed just as I was preparing to burst in upon the scene and steal her away.

From Barcelona she went to France, on the arms of a burly Frenchman. I caught up with them in Paris as they shopped on the Boulevard des Rêvers. How stealthily I stalked them as they went from store to store, emerging from each laden with packages, the price of her love, no doubt. And it was on that boulevard where I decided to make my move. The Frenchman was standing in front of Jacqueline's Jewelry Store, unable to enter for he was weighed down with a mountain of packages. I laughed out loud as he handed her a fistful of bills with which to make any further purchases herself. I watched the Frenchman put down the packages, slowly, carefully, so that nothing was disturbed. Then he pulled out a handkerchief and wiped his brow. He was red in the face from his exertions. Little did he know that his real exertion was about to begin.

I approached nonchalantly and asked what had brought him to such a state. He replied animatedly about this jewel of a woman he had discovered while vacationing in Barcelona, of the marvelous gifts she had brought to the table of his love, and how, after having been with her merely a weekend, he could not imagine being with another. He pulled his handkerchief out and dabbed at his eyes, which were filled with tears.

"She sounds like a remarkable woman," I said, as he finished his peroration. "Indeed, you are a lucky man."

He sighed with self-satisfaction and grinned from ear to ear.

"But I fear there may be a false note in this lovely duet," I continued. "Only several blocks back I passed an alleyway and—I swear—I saw a woman meeting your lover's description satisfying most directly the desires of another man." I pointed in the direction from which I had come.

"That's impossible!" he cried. "I saw her go into this store. I've been waiting here the entire time."

"It would be easy for her to slip away unnoticed. Only look at this mountain of packages which surrounds you. Why, you cannot even see the storefront."

He turned around and saw that this was true.

"How long have you been waiting?" I asked.

He looked at his watch. "Five, perhaps ten, minutes."

I shook my head sadly. "That would have given her just enough time."

"How dare she do this! I who bought her all you see before you." He pointed at the packages.

"You know how women are," I said. I paused, then inflicted my final wound: "I am afraid, sir, that she has made of you an ass."

The man jumped to his feet and cried:

"Le Guillotine! Le Guillotine!" and ran off in the direction I had pointed, leaving me free to confront my beloved.

I took a deep breath, opened the door to Jacqueline's Jewelry Store, and walked inside.

I saw my beloved leaning over a counter near the front of the store, examining a string of pearls. I went up to the counter and tapped her on the shoulder. She turned around and her mouth dropped open in amazement.

"Well, I'll be," she said. "Look who's here!"

Extending a long arm, I reached behind the counter, scooped up the pearls, placed them around her neck, and once again proposed marriage.

She giggled—not the violent reaction I'd expected—chewed on her thumbnail for nearly a minute and, finally, answered:

"I won't marry you, Jonathan. But I shall go off with you on an adventure!"

And laughing like the wily seductress that she was, she took one of my hands and pulled me towards the door.

"Consider them a gift to the goddess of Love," I said to the store clerk who, pointing at the pearls, vainly tried to block our exit.

* * *

Mount Hipurtya is a ten-thousand-foot peak located in the Andes Mountains in Central Peru. Famous for the verticality of its slopes, the depth of its chasms, the spontaneity of its avalanches, it was so far unscaled by mankind. A climb to the top was not exactly the adventure I had in mind, but I would be with my beloved, nothing else mattered.

Louis Mecharde was to be our guide. My beloved told me she had found him while vacationing in the south of France. He was known the world over for his skill as a mountain climber, she said, and had led expeditions to various peaks in the Andes. If I'd paid attention to the gleam that came into her eyes when she spoke of Louis, I might have thought twice about what we were about to embark upon, but I did not notice.

My beloved told me she had unfinished business to attend to in Norway and sent me on ahead. She arrived in Lima two weeks later and we were joined by Louis the week after that. Lima was a wonderful place, full of energy, song, and dance—a never-ending carnival. I will forever treasure the memories of me and my beloved parading through the center of town, dancing until dawn, kissing in a park like two youths introducing themselves to the pleasures of love. We became known throughout Lima as "that lovely young couple" in the week before we began our upward journey. I, in turn, found the residents of Lima both gracious and hospitable. The perfect hosts to entertain the perfect guests.

Our ascent began on a cool, crisp June day. Half of Lima followed us to the mountain's base to give us a merry send-off. A brass band played, jugglers juggled, young girls danced. And as we started up, with Louis leading the way, me and my beloved arm in arm, a thousand balloons were released into the air—red, purple, green, and white—it was a magnificent occasion!

The climb proceeded effortlessly. Louis was a master guide. One-thousand, two-thousand, three-thousand feet. We pitched our tents for the night. Four-thousand, five-thousand, six-thousand feet. The view was stupendous, the air rarefied and pure. I saw animals I had never seen before: strange antelope-like creatures with half a dozen horns protruding from their heads and weasels that darted to and fro and I saw birds which sang to me in strange tongues. Such a wonderful, marvelous adventure which would only have been better if my beloved had let me make love to her. But *still* she would not. Indeed, she slept now in Louis's tent. To protect herself, she teased, from me and my animal desires.

Seven-thousand, eight-thousand feet. I was at peace with myself. I saw no more animals, heard not a single avian. All was silent around me, an eerie, eternal silence such as I had never experienced. (Louis and my beloved were rarely with me now; indeed, they seemed to disappear for hours on end.)

Nine-thousand feet. A wide assortment of flora covered the mountainside, magnificent flowers that filled the scene with beauty. Red Peruvian sundew and purple lupine. Orange cactus thistle and yellow dandelion nestled amongst swaying grass. Acres and acres of mountain fern and—most wondrous of all—rare Pichu bamboo with its long slender branches and delicate leaves. I wondered if I was climbing not a mountain but a stairway to the gates of Heaven so wondrous had my journey become.

Ten-thousand feet. I reached the peak at last! And there I saw my beloved, on Louis's arm, laughing as if she were inebriated, though of course she was only intoxicated by the incredible sights and sounds around her.

And then! And then! And then! My beloved came to me one night; I was alone in my tent. She snuggled up to me; I stroked her cheeks; her skin was soft, smooth, supple. We made love then, a love so passionate you could have heard the angels sing. I nearly died of happiness at that moment, for the ambitions of a lifetime were fulfilled. And when we finished, many hours after we had begun, I drifted off into a blissful sleep, the sleep of a newborn child after it has suckled at its mother's breast.

I awoke the next morning to find myself alone. I burst into tears, realizing it had been but a dream. My beloved had run off with Louis, apparently, for they were nowhere to be found. But where had they gone? To enjoy the magnificent mountaintop view? To dance through a field of flowers? To bathe in a nearby stream? It was then I noticed a piece of paper taped to the side of my tent. As I expected, it was a message from my beloved:

My dearest Jonathon:

Louis has asked me to accompany him on a safari in Central Africa and I have accepted. I am so excited. Can you picture me at a watering hole with the elephants, rhinos, and gazelles? It will be the adventure of a lifetime!

Thanks for coming with me on this little journey and thanks for all the kind words you have bestowed upon me. I am perfect? No, I am far from perfect. But neither do I wish to be perfect; for I realize that a life fully lived is a life filled with imperfections, a life of continually overcoming imperfection. . . .

Your far-from-perfect-but-ever-adventurous-friend,

Marie

The sarcasm literally dripped off the paper, the hatred, the anger, the venom! I cursed her aloud, crumpled the note into a ball, and threw it to the ground. Enraged like a wounded bull I howled to the heavens, "Oh cruel, cruel world how can she treat me this way, I who loved her as no man ever loved before?" I saw *in her* the perfect lover? It was quite the opposite: I had offered *to her* the perfect love. Yet now, as I considered her behavior, I saw that she was hardly beyond reproach. Her own faults were many. But nothing—nothing—was more telling than this: men the world over had admired her, fallen for her, pursued her, even tasted her love, but it was me and me alone who realized she was *not* the perfect woman. Had none of my previous actions indicated my perfection this one certainly did.

In a word, my beloved was a tart, not worthy of my attention. The perfect love I had so desperately sought was still out there, waiting to be found. *But my own perfection was not in question; indeed, I held myself in higher regard than ever before.*

I packed up my tent and started down the mountain, comforted by these latest revelations, and a week later came upon our base camp. In appearance I was hungry, shivering, alone, but inwardly I was filled with the warmth that the knowledge of my own sainthood had given me. I was greeted by the roaring applause and thunderous ovations of the residents of Lima who, realizing my return was imminent, had gathered at the foot of the mountain to welcome me back to society, to welcome me back as a god descending from the mountaintop, a god who, kindly and with overwhelming compassion, would greet his followers waiting patiently below.

WHAT HAPPENED TO VINCENT GUTBOMB ONE DAY

When Vincent Gutbomb awoke one morning and glanced at the clock on the bedside table, he saw that it was earlier than usual. He sat half-up in bed and rubbed his eyes. Had he been awakened by unpleasant dreams? Or was he simply jittery over his upcoming presentation? He was to give a talk that morning, precisely at nine o'clock, to his boss and several other department heads. The talk was entitled: "The Future of the Worker: An Evolutionary Approach." He thought it quite good—and certain to send his reputation soaring. No, he was not worried about the presentation—or anything else for that matter. He had been sleeping soundly—just like a babe. At least as far as he could tell.

Just then he realized someone was knocking at the door. He jumped up from the bed and pulled on his clothes.

"Who is it?" he asked, startled. Why would anyone come to see him at this hour?

Another knock, followed by a hard kick.

Trembling, Gutbomb cracked open the door and peeked out.

"Yes?"

The door was pushed open in his face and a man barged inside. Gutbomb stepped back. The man was in his early fifties, dressed in a dark, three-piece suit, and had black hair which looked suspiciously like a toupee. His eyes were dark blue, his nose a long, Italian one; his mouth was drawn in a bitter expression.

"Your name?" snapped the man.

"Vincent Gutbomb."

"Aha! I thought as much!"

The man reached into his coat pocket and pulled out a card. "My credentials," he said, holding out the card for Gutbomb's inspection.

The card indicated the man was a lawyer.

"You must have confused me with someone else," Gutbomb said. "I, certainly, haven't requested your services."

The lawyer stared at Gutbomb solemnly. Then he said:

"I'm here to take your case."

Gutbomb knew he was not on trial, had no cases pending; why, he was not even under suspicion of a crime. Had this person confused him with someone else? It seemed unlikely—this "lawyer" seemed certain he had found his man. Maybe he was simply one of the bizarre street people who frequented Gutbomb's neighborhood.

"It's hard to say what your chances are," the lawyer continued. "Your case is delicate, you know, full of legalistic traps and pitfalls. In cases of your kind it's doubtful whether one has any chance at all. Even so, you mustn't despair; that's my job: to keep you from despairing. As for your chances per se, if we assume, as we must, that they do in fact exist, then why worry? A million-to-one shot is better than nothing and anything that's better than nothing is something, so we do have something and that's a start. To sum up, then, I would say your chances are something."

"And something is better than nothing."

"Of course."

"But I'm innocent."

"Innocent? Ha! You're as guilty as the next man."

"And how guilty is he?"

"As guilty as you." The lawyer smiled.

It must be said that the more Gutbomb listened to the lawyer the more he began to wonder: perhaps he had dismissed the man too quickly. He spoke with such a determined and confident air and his resonant voice echoed throughout Gutbomb's apartment like thunder. He must have been a wonder to behold in the courtroom.

It was true that Gutbomb had been preoccupied with work of late, perhaps he had not noticed a recent summons he'd received. And if that was the case perhaps the man before him was the court appointed lawyer. He decided it best to take the matter seriously: no point in taking chances with the law.

"You say you're my lawyer."

"Correct."

"And you say I'm guilty."

"Correct."

"Why are you defending me if I'm guilty?"

"I'm defending you."

"But why? Why defend people who are guilty?"

"Why do I do it?"

"Yes."

"Out of boredom."

"You're bored with my case?"

"Sure," the lawyer replied, shrugging his shoulders. "You're guilty; what's there to look forward to?"

"My innocence?"

"But you're guilty! I thought we'd established that."

"We still haven't established what I'm supposedly guilty of."

The lawyer laughed. "Don't you know?"

Gutbomb stomped his feet in anger. "My guilt—what am I guilty of?"

The lawyer giggled. "Nothing."

"Nothing?"

"Absolutely nothing."

"Absolutely nothing?"

"Positively, absolutely nothing."

"That's preposterous! If I'm guilty of nothing—why, then I'm innocent!"

The lawyer laughed. "It's a good thing I'm your lawyer," he said. "That defense would never stand up in court."

"What do you want from me?" Gutbomb said. He was beginning to wonder if he may have been correct the first time: perhaps this "lawyer" really was just some weird alley bum.

"I want your confession."

"My confession? You said you're my lawyer; you're supposed to defend me."

"True, I'm your lawyer. But I can't defend you unless I know you're guilty."

"That makes as much sense as—"

"It doesn't make any sense at all."

"Then why did you say it?"

"Say what?"

"That you can't defend me."

"I said that?"

"Yes, you did. You said—"

"Look," continued the lawyer. "Obviously, if I'm going to defend you I must believe I can obtain your acquittal."

"Then you believe in my innocence."

"I didn't say that."

"But you admit the possibility."

"Why should I do that?"

"You said you can obtain my acquittal."

"It's impossible."

Gutbomb threw his hands over his head in dismay. "But you just said—"

The lawyer sighed. "What I just said bears no relevance to the present situation. What I just said bore relevance only to the point of time in which I said it, but now that time is past; it no longer has relevance. In fact, what I just said about what I just said no longer has relevance, so you can forget that, too." He paused. "But then again, what I just said about what I just said about what I just said no longer has relevance either and it's quite possible that what I said in the first place does have relevance, except of course that what I just said about what I said in the first place no longer has relevance."

"Which leaves me?"

"Innocent." The lawyer grinned.

"But you said I'm guilty!"

"Yes, you're as guilty as you'll ever be. In fact, you haven't the slightest bit of hope left."

"And even so, you want to be my lawyer?"

"Correct." Up to this point the lawyer had been staring intently at Gutbomb; now he began fidgeting with the buttons on his suit jacket.

Gutbomb continued, "And you're convinced of my guilt?"

"That too is correct," the lawyer replied, continuing to play with his jacket.

"There's one thing I don't understand," said Gutbomb. "If you're convinced of my guilt, why do you need my confession?"

"It's necessary for your defense."

Gutbomb scowled. This was going nowhere. He would try a new line of questioning:

"How many others have you represented?"

"I'm not sure; I lost track some time ago."

"How many were found guilty?"

"Why, they always were guilty."

"Then you've lost all your cases."

"Of course I've lost them. Certainly, you don't expect a guilty man to be found innocent."

"But why did you defend them in the first place? If you knew they would be found guilty . . ."

"Obviously, I hoped to obtain their acquittal."

"But you failed."

"Of course I did. How could I obtain their acquittal if they were guilty?"

"Nevertheless, in my case you think that you can."

"I do."

"And you further assert that I'm guilty."

"As guilty as the next man."

"And if you lose?"

"You will suffer the same punishment as the others."

"And what was their punishment?"

"They were turned into vegetables." The lawyer grinned.

"But that means—"

"Now hold on," the lawyer interrupted. "I've one button left to unfasten; it will just take a second—"

"But—"

"There!" He opened his jacket to reveal a leather portfolio, and he held it up for Gutbomb's inspection. "Now we can proceed with the particulars." He opened the portfolio and spread its contents over the floor. Gutbomb bent down to get a closer look: they seemed to be charts or graphs.

"What do these figures mean?" Gutbomb pointed at the papers.

"I haven't the faintest idea."

"You've never seen them before?"

"Hardly. I made them up myself."

This was more than even Gutbomb could bear. "I've heard enough twiddle-twaddle," he said. "It's time for you to leave."

"No, no, no!" cried the lawyer in alarm. "Let's talk this over. Perhaps you feel you've been placed under too much of a strain. That's understandable; most of my clients have felt that way at one time or another. It will pass, I assure you. If it makes you feel better, I don't feel so well myself. A fainting spell seems to be coming over me. Perhaps I need a glass of water. Yes, a glass of cold water sounds just right. Could I have a glass of water?"

Gutbomb reached into his back pocket and pulled out the lawyer's card. "I refuse to accept your services," he said. "I'm dismissing you from the case." He ripped up the card and threw the pieces into the air.

The lawyer stepped back and held up his arms in protest. "Surely you jest!"

"I assure you I'm quite serious."

"True, your case is hopeless and you're as guilty as the next man and your acquittal will be impossible to obtain and in the end you'll be turned into a veg—"

"I appreciate your taking an interest in my case. But I'm too busy right now with work-related matters to become involved in what is obviously an intricate legal case. For one thing, I would never have time to explore the many legalistic ramifications which are sure to arise."

The lawyer looked at Gutbomb as if Gutbomb were an imbecile. "But that's my job," he said.

"I'm sorry."

The lawyer sighed. "As you wish." He stooped to gather the papers and he stuffed them into the portfolio. Then he rose and walked to the door. "You're certain you don't want to reconsider?"

"My decision is final."

The lawyer looked Gutbomb over slowly from head to toe. He opened his mouth as if to protest a final time, then thought better of it, shrugged his shoulders, and disappeared.

Gutbomb sighed; finally he was free. He looked at the clock on the bedside table—and he nearly fainted. It was eight forty-five. Fifteen minutes until his presentation—and his office was a good twenty-minute walk away!

He had a more immediate problem, however: how to exit the room? The hallway was out of the question. If that lawyer saw him—who knew what might happen. Ah, there was one other way: the window! He hadn't opened it since he'd painted the room several months ago. It might be stuck shut. That was all he needed! He unhooked the window lock and tried to push the window open. Just as he feared: it would not budge.

* * *

Vincent Gutbomb was a writer. The workaday world bored him, but there was nothing he could do about it—

he had to make a living. And so at night, after the day's labors, he would retire to his apartment and compose fairy tales and romance novels, vignettes about the common folk and their daily struggles, stories that took place in other times and places, times and places that only he, Vincent Gutbomb, could imagine.

Unfortunately, there were times—he could not deny it—when he was so involved with a literary creation that he could not keep his mind on his office duties. He was absent-minded—to be blunt—and he might forget—for a while—about this task or that one—he would remember later of course, no harm done, but it had landed him in hot water on more than one occasion. Why, once he had even been threatened with dismissal.

* * *

Gutbomb pulled out his pocketknife, hoping he could slice through the paint, when . . .

Knock! Knock! Knock!

He froze.

Knock! Knock! Knock!

He went to the door and opened it gingerly.

"I thought I made myself clear—" he began but stopped short. The man facing him was not the lawyer. He was wearing a sparkling white suit, studded with diamonds; around his neck hung a brilliant diamond necklace. Dark glasses hid his eyes from view.

"My credentials," the man said, pushing a card through the doorway.

Gutbomb snapped up the card. It indicated the man was an undertaker.

"I'm sorry," said Gutbomb with a harumph. "There are no dead men here."

"That's what you think!" cried the undertaker, pushing open the door and brushing past Gutbomb brusquely. He strode into the middle of the room and then wheeled around and exclaimed, "I'm here for you."

Gutbomb was aghast. "For me? I'm not dead."

"Oh, I know that. You're innocent."

"Innocent!" Gutbomb practically shouted the word. Now this matter could be cleared up quickly. But then a look of confusion crossed his. "If you believe I'm innocent," he said, "why are you here?"

"I'm here to finalize the arrangements."

"What arrangements?"

The undertaker smiled. "What dirt do you wish to be covered with?"

"Dirt? What are you talking about?"

"Personally, I think brown dirt would suit you best. You have your choice, of course, among brown, black, red, yellow, orange, pink, or our new color called Gutbombian."

Gutbomb frowned. "Are you in cahoots with the lawyer?"

"I despise the man. In fact, I cringe whenever I see him."

"You must have seen him just now."

"As a matter of fact I did. I was walking down the hallway when I saw the lawyer storm out of your apartment. It was then I realized his mission had been a failure. But bother all that—which color shall it be?"

"The lawyer said I was guilty," replied Gutbomb. "And you?"

"I think you should pick a color."

"You're as crazy as the lawyer," Gutbomb said in dismay. "He says I'm guilty and you say I'm innocent and I say you're both mad."

"And I say pick a color."

"A color of what?"

"A color of dirt."

"What do I have to do with the dirt?"

"It's not what you have to do with the dirt; it's why you have to do with the dirt." The undertaker grinned; his teeth sparkled like diamonds.

"And why do I have to do with the dirt?"

"Because you're innocent."

"You mean, all innocent people have to do with the dirt."

"Yes. It's quite simple, isn't it?"

"It's exasperating if you ask me." For several minutes neither said a word; all the while the undertaker fidgeted with his pockets. Then Gutbomb continued, "You say all innocent people have to do with the dirt. But you haven't said what all innocent people have to do with the dirt. That is, you haven't said what the dirt that all innocent people have to do with does to the people who have to do with it."

"It's used to bury people."

"You want to bury me?! Why?"

"Because you're innocent. All innocent people must be buried; it's inherent to their nature of being innocent."

"You wish to kill me?!"

"Don't put it so harshly. I will dig a hole in the ground just big enough to fit a man of your measurements and you will get into it and I will cover you with dirt. Not much mind you; not even enough to form a small mound, just enough to cover you completely."

"That's ridiculous!" cried Gutbomb. "Why, a person could simply get up and walk away!"

"In that case they were not innocent to begin with; they were only pretending to be innocent."

"What person would stand idly by while someone else put him in a hole and covered him with dirt?"

"An innocent one."

"I don't understand. You let guilty people walk around scot-free and you put innocent people in holes and cover them with dirt?!"

"I see nothing odd in that. Surely you wouldn't protest if it was the other way around."

"But it isn't."

"Who's to say it isn't? It depends on the way you look at it. Guilt is relative to innocence and innocence is relative to guilt. That is: they're simply words; if we say 'guilt' is 'innocence'—"

Gutbomb was too confused at this point to reply.

The undertaker continued, "You still haven't told me what color of dirt you wish to be covered with."

"I don't want any color," replied Gutbomb. "I'm not innocent."

"Not innocent?" The undertaker frowned.

"I'm not guilty either."

"That's impossible. You're either guilty or innocent; the two are all encompassing. That's the beauty of it."

"What's beautiful about putting innocent people in holes and letting guilty people roam free?"

The undertaker shook his head. "You're simply having a case of the jitters. It is, admittedly, rare in cases of innocence; but I'm sure it's the reason for your present behavior. It will pass, I assure you." He paused and began searching his pockets. "Ah, here we are," he said, pulling out a tape measure. He drew near Gutbomb and wrapped the tape around the poor man's waist.

"What are you doing?" asked Gutbomb, instinctively retreating.

"I'm taking your measurements. I can't dig the proper size hole unless I have your correct measurements."

"I've had enough of this!" Gutbomb cried as he pulled away the tape measure. If the truth be told, he was scared. He pushed the undertaker into the hallway and shut the door, throwing the lock as he did so.

For the third time that day Gutbomb looked at the clock—and this time he had to force himself to do so, for he knew that the time for his presentation had certainly passed. It was half-past nine. Even so there was hope. Probably the directors were sitting around a conference table, drinking coffee and reveling in the latest company news: which marketing strategies were in and which were out, which products were in and which were out, which managers were in and which were out. If Gutbomb were to hurry, he might make it to work in fifteen minutes; he would only be forty-five minutes late; with a bit of explaining he might be forgiven. And when they heard his marvelous presentation—then all would be forgiven and forgotten for sure!

The path to the window was clear. Several cuts with a penknife to pry away the dried paint and the window opened easily. Gutbomb pulled himself through and jumped to the alley below.

The alleyway opened onto a lifeless street. The sky was tinged a bizarre yellow color, giving it an appearance Gutbomb had never seen before. Everything around him was eerily quiet. A feeling of dread closed in upon him. He tried to shrug it off but was unable to do so. He took a deep breath and plunged ahead.

"What are you doing?"

He looked around in disbelief. From out of nowhere had appeared six elderly gentlemen wearing black suits. Their figures were lean, their faces grim. They stared at him menacingly. What did they want?

"What's going on?" Gutbomb said.

"That's what we asked you," spoke up one of them, pointing first to himself and then to Gutbomb. The others indicated their agreement.

"You're linked to the lawyer and the undertaker, aren't you?"

"He thinks we're linked to the lawyer and the undertaker," said one of them, evoking howls of laughter from the others.

"He thinks we've been looking for him," said another, giggling loudly.

"Don't deny it," Gutbomb continued. "Who are you here for if not for me?"

"We are here for you."

"I know!" Gutbomb cried. "You're my jury!"

For a moment they were silent, then one said:

"Of course we're your jury."

"And you're the foreman." Gutbomb pointed to the man who had just spoken.

"No, I'm the foreman," said another and, in truth, his features were more refined than the others. "Yes, I'm the foreman," he repeated, "And I'm here to announce our verdict."

"A majority decision I hope."

"A unanimous decision."

"A unanimous decision!"

"We had no trouble agreeing." The foreman spoke crisply, pronouncing his words with a diplomatic air.

"What then is your verdict?"

"You are innocent."

"Innocent? This is too much!" cried Gutbomb. "Only moments ago I was convinced of my guilt; now all has changed." He stopped short when he realized something wasn't right and he looked from one solemn face to another. "What's wrong?" he asked. "I am free! You are free! Your work is done!" Their faces were unchanged.

"He doesn't seem to understand," said the foreman. The others nodded in agreement.

"Doesn't understand? You've told me I'm innocent. What more is there to say?" Gutbomb took a step forward, but they did not give way. "What are you doing? I can leave if I want to."

"We're here to arrest you," they said in unison.

"Arrest me? But you said I was innocent."

"You are."

"But why arrest me if I'm innocent?" Gutbomb pointed to the foreman, "You said I was innocent."

"You are."

"Yet you want to arrest me?"

"We do."

"On what charge?"

"I believe I made myself clear. I said we were arresting you for being innocent; and it's not a 'charge' but a 'conviction.' The convicted must understand this; it's necessary for his defense."

"I don't understand. You said I was convicted."

"You have been convicted. But you'll need to defend your past acts of innocence. Plead temporary insanity; your case will be dismissed immediately. As long as you understand that your past acts of innocence were caused by periods of insanity, you have nothing to fear. You will be found guilty of innocence since, as far as you are concerned, you are guilty of innocence—"

"But I'm innocent."

"I admire your courage. It's not easy for a convicted man to repent so promptly. You've just made the first step towards a full realization of guilt of innocence."

"But I'm not guilty of anything."

"You're guilty of innocence."

"Innocence carries no guilt. Don't you understand? I'm not 'repenting' anything. I'm innocent of guilt. All guilt! I refuse to plead guilty of innocence."

"He doesn't understand," said the foreman to the others, who responded with loud guffaws. The foreman turned to Gutbomb and said, "Let me explain once again. We the jury have found you guilty of innocence and hereby arrest you in the name of the law."

"My trial!" cried Gutbomb, clapping his hands in glee. "Tell me about my trial. I missed it, you know, for I was meditating on the nature of guilt and innocence at the time and I forgot all about it. How did it go? Were there arguments in my defense? Did the gallery cheer when my name was announced? Did young girls weep when my conviction was decided? Please, tell me. I am eager to know."

"You should be ashamed of yourself," said the foreman, shaking his head.

"Ashamed of what? Tell me and I'll repent."

"The way you treated the lawyer. The poor man was heartbroken at your refusal to admit your guilt. Nevertheless, he gave a moving speech on your behalf. At one point he broke down and wept. I still recall the power he commanded: staring wrathfully, gesticulating wildly, kicking the bench in anger. We were moved, to say the least. But an acquittal was not to be. The lawyer had just finished and the gallery was applauding wildly when in stormed the undertaker—"

"The undertaker!"

"A most despicable man." The others nodded in agreement and straightened their suits. "He stormed in and insisted that he, too, should be allowed to plead your case. Without waiting for us to consider his proposal, he took to the floor and began sputtering absurd rhetoric. Supposedly it related to your case; but we could make nothing of it."

"What verdict did he ask for?" interrupted Gutbomb.

"He asked that you be found innocent of guilt—"

"Innocent!"

"—and as a reward be placed in a hole and covered with dirt."

Gutbomb groaned.

"That's how we felt." The others nodded in agreement and straightened their suits. "We told him such a verdict was impossible; but he refused to listen and continued with his speech. Then the lawyer interrupted and the two exchanged insults. The abusive language they used! We'd never heard anything like it, and in a courtroom besides!" The other jurors shook their heads and brought their fingers to their lips: tsk! tsk! tsk! they said. "The gallery was shocked; scattered 'boos' filled the air. 'Gentlemen, control yourselves,' I cried, but they refused to listen and continued hurling verbal hatchets in all directions—by now, they were yelling not only at each other, but also at the gallery, even at the jury itself. The courtroom was ready to explode. I banged my gavel and—"

Gutbomb looked confused. "Where was the judge?" he interjected.

"The judge? Why, he was off with the stenographer; they're having an affair, you know. It's been going on for some time; seems he's really fallen for the lady—though there are others—"

"Others?"

"I'd say there are three or four women he's presently involved with. It varies with the season."

"Doesn't that interfere with his work?"

"Of course it does. You don't think he has time to devote to the court when he's chasing women, do you? I'd say he hasn't been in the courtroom for at least a year; except for the time he was caught beneath the stenographer's desk when the court was in session."

"And you let this behavior persist?"

"What else can we do?"

"You could impeach him."

"Oh, that would never do; he's the judge."

"What does that have to do with it?"

"Everything. He's the judge and if he wants to run around with women he can do so. Impeachment would only complicate the issue, as we would have to hold another election and—"

"What's wrong with that? It seems the logical thing to do."

"No, no, no," replied the foreman, shaking his head. "It would never work. You seem to consider the judge's behavior unusual when in fact it is nothing out of the ordinary. It happens all the time; in fact, it's expected of him. Maybe if he did not act the way he does, maybe then we would consider impeachment, but not until."

"You mean all government officials act this way?"

"I wouldn't say all, for I have contact only with the judicial department. There it is common practice and takes up much of an employee's time"—at this point the foreman hung his head and blushed—"I must confess that lately I've been seeing the stenographer's daughter, a lovely young girl of sixteen. But in no way does it interfere with my duties. In fact, of late I've been filling in for the judge, as I did at your trial. I believe that prompted your original question, as you were wondering why the judge was not present."

"It did concern me."

"As well it should have. But as I said before, I had taken over his duties so there was nothing for you to fear. As for me, however, the situation was different. I had a crisis on my hands—the situation between the lawyer and the undertaker—and it was growing worse by the minute. I banged my gavel and ordered them back to their seats. At first they ignored me and carried on as before. 'Gentlemen!' I cried. 'Please, be seated. We will rule on this case immediately.' My words had no effect: their insults only grew louder. One of them call me an 'egg-headed judge,' a remark which upset me greatly, for I don't consider my head to be shaped like an egg, do you?" Gutbomb nodded in agreement. "Yes, it upset me greatly. I replied with a remark equally offensive, but it seemed only to anger them further. 'Gentlemen, please!' I exclaimed a third time; still nothing. I hurled my gavel at them; it landed to one side and rebounded high into the gallery. The lawyer and the undertaker looked up startled. 'Please be seated,' I said. They did as I asked. 'We will now rule on the case.' Once again I was interrupted, this time by the undertaker. 'I wasn't finished,' he said, in a whimpering, childish voice. 'Shut up you filthy bastard!' I replied, rising menacingly from the bench. He quieted down then but continued to whimper."

"What pleas did they enter?" interrupted Gutbomb. "I feel it's central to my case."

"And indeed it is. The lawyer entered a plea of 'guilty of guilt,' the undertaker a plea of 'innocent of guilt.' We deliberated for nearly three hours and finally came up with our verdict: guilty—"

"Of innocence."

"Correct."

"But that wasn't one of the alternatives."

"Why must it have been one of the alternatives? The defense is free to enter any plea it wants, but we don't have to consider it when reaching our verdict. We make up our own and throw out or redesign those of the defense at will. Pleas are superficial, what really matters are the facts—"

"That makes sense."

"—and the facts cannot be changed—"

"That make sense."

"—therefore your guilt or innocence cannot change—"

"That makes sense."

"—therefore we can ignore it."

"Ignore what?"

"The facts."

"What??"

"We can ignore the facts, since you are either guilty or innocent and no matter how we change the facts you are still either guilty or innocent."

"Not if you change the facts."

"The facts have nothing to do with your guilt or innocence, for your guilt or innocence has already been determined and is therefore irrevocably fixed in the ever-running ticker tape of time."

"Then why change them?"

"We change the facts to look at your case from all possible angles since only by looking at your case from all possible angles can we determine your guilt or innocence. We change a fact and ask 'what would he have done in this situation?' and we juxtapose that with the actual fact to see how they differ. We do this repeatedly and come up with a complete set of actions and reactions and from it draw our verdict."

"But my actual guilt or innocence remains the same no matter what you do."

"True—the entire procedure is meaningless."

"Then why do you do it?"

"We have to answer to the court."

"I don't understand."

"We must present the court with a verdict. It is written that this must be done."

"How, then, did the court react?"

"The reaction was overwhelmingly in our favor, the only sore spot having to do with the undertaker; he acted like a child. Upon hearing the verdict he jumped up and cried: 'We'll appeal! We'll appeal!' Then he began swearing profusely. I tried to quiet him, but he only cursed louder and then burst into tears. 'Please, Mr. Undertaker', I said, 'try not to take this so emotionally; no one else cares.' By this time his tears had turned into convulsions and he was beating the floor with his fists. 'Really, Mr. Undertaker,' I said, 'isn't this carrying things too far?' Now he was frothing at the mouth and clutching frantically at his throat. I thought he was trying to strangle himself. I was on the verge of reversing the verdict myself just to appease him, when he jumped up, uttered a cry, and ran up into the gallery, where his sobs were lost among the cheers of—"

"Cheers?"

"The moment the verdict was announced, the gallery burst into thunderous applause. Balloons and confetti were everywhere. A regular madhouse if ever I've seen one."

"And you let the lawyer and the undertaker be subjected to that ridicule? Losing the case was punishment enough, but allowing all that—"

"What does the lawyer have to do with any of this?"

"Well, he must have been upset too—"

"He was overjoyed. He was cheering louder than the others. It was the culmination of a lifetime. The pinnacle of a career. The zenith of success. The—"

"But he didn't receive the verdict he asked for. He entered a plea of 'guilty of guilt' and you returned a verdict of 'guilty of innocence'—those are opposites."

"Opposites?" The foreman laughed. "Why, they're nearly identical, maybe a minor difference, but nothing to get concerned about. Now, Mr. Undertaker's plea was opposite: 'innocent of guilt' is opposite to 'guilty of innocence,' the verdict we returned."

"I'll grant you that," said Gutbomb. "But the lawyer's plea was also opposite."

"How can two opposites be opposite to something else?" said the foreman. "Examine the pleas they entered: 'innocent of guilt' by Mr. Undertaker, and 'guilty of guilt' by Mr. Lawyer. Both are indicating opposite states regarding your guilt, are they not?"

"Yes, that is true."

"Therefore, they are opposites."

"I'll grant you that."

"Now, the verdict we returned was 'guilty of innocence'—"

"Correct."

"—which is opposite to 'innocent of guilt' but nearly identical to 'guilty of guilt.' Therefore, it was only natural for Mr. Undertaker to weep hysterically and for Mr. Lawyer to cheer wildly."

"No, no, no. Your logic is flawed. The undertaker's plea of 'innocent of guilt' is opposite to your verdict of 'guilty of innocence.' But the lawyer's plea of 'guilty of guilt' is also opposite to your verdict." The foreman started to protest, but Gutbomb cut him off. "In fact, there are three opposites at work. The undertaker's plea of 'innocent of guilt' is also opposite to the lawyer's plea of 'guilty of guilt,' though in a way opposite to both other opposites. Thus, what we have here is a situation of three opposites, each opposite to the others in an opposite way."

"No, no, no," said the foreman. "It is your logic which is flawed. We returned a verdict of 'guilty of innocence.' Mr. Undertaker was upset with that verdict, therefore his plea was opposite to our verdict. Furthermore, Mr. Lawyer was happy with the verdict, therefore his plea was similar to our verdict. If Mr. Lawyer had been upset with the verdict, his plea would have been opposite to the verdict. His plea, however, was not opposite to the verdict and therefore he was happy with the verdict."

"That doesn't make any sense and you know it!" snapped Gutbomb.

"I think that's one of the most sensible statements I've ever made."

"That's it!" shouted Gutbomb. "I've had all the double talk from you I'm going to take."

"I'm sorry you feel that way—" began the foreman, but Gutbomb interrupted:

"Take your five giggly friends and leave at once."

"He doesn't understand," said the foreman to the others, who had shrunk back in fright upon hearing Gutbomb's remark.

"Doesn't understand what?" said Gutbomb and then answered his own question, "Oh, that's right, I'm under arrest aren't I? 'Guilty of innocence,' you say. I suppose my punishment comes next."

"Yes, I suppose that it does." The foreman turned towards the others and said: "Don't you think Mr. Gutbomb deserves to be punished?"

The five jurors grinned as they straightened their suits.

Gutbomb said, "I'm not even sure they know what we've been talking about."

"I beg your pardon," cried the foreman, "They've been following our conversation with the utmost scrutiny. It's their duty as jurors to examine all the facts."

"I don't care what their duty is," replied Gutbomb. "They're ignorant fools who can't see the facts to examine them." The five jurors winced as if in pain and sobbed meekly.

"I think I know what your problem is," the foreman said. "It's common for the newly arrested to experience feelings of confusion and despair. Try to remain calm; these feelings will soon—"

"I've heard enough of your nonsense," snapped Gutbomb. And with that he pushed his way past the jurors and started down the street.

The big clock on the town hall read ten forty. He would be at work by eleven—just in time to receive his pink slip. He had been warned about his tardiness before. Once more and you're out, Gutbomb, they had said. You and your foolish stories.

What would they think of his latest excuse? A lawyer? An undertaker? A jury? This is the last straw, they would say. You're nothing but an absent-minded buffoon. You'll never amount to anything in the literary world. Time to get back to the daily grind!

But if only they knew what had happened. If only they would believe him this time. Life was full of weird episodes, strange happenings, unimaginable events. If only they would give him one more chance.

And to Gutbomb's surprise, not a single member of the jury made a move to stop him. But their laughter was still echoing in his ears as he disappeared around the corner.

About the Author

Brian Biswas has published dozens of stories in the United States as well as internationally. He is the author of the short story collection *A Betrayal and Other Stories* and the novel *The Astronomer*. He writes in a literary style reminiscent of magical realism which attempts to convey a slightly exaggerated but internally consistent sense of reality. He also writes gothic or neo-gothic tales, and straightforward horror and science fiction stories, often tinged with fantastic elements.

Brian was born in Columbus, Ohio. He received a B.A. in Philosophy from Antioch College in Yellow Springs, Ohio, and an M.S. in Computer Science from the University of Illinois at Urbana-Champaign. He lives in an old neighborhood in Chapel Hill, North Carolina with his wife, Elizabeth, and an ever-changing assortment of animals.